SUPERnaturals

AMONG CAROLINA FOLK AND THEIR NEIGHBORS

By

F. ROY JOHNSON

Illustrated By

JUDY GODWIN MIZELLE

JOHNSON PUBLISHING COMPANY

Murfreesboro, N. C., 27855

094930

Copyright 1974
F. Roy Johnson
All Rights Reserved

Contents

I
THE TRADITIONAL HERITAGE

1. Rich and Diverse Traditions 9

II
ACTS OF PROVIDENCE

2. The Workings of Providence 17
3. Warnings 18
4. Messages 25
5. Judgments Suspended 29
6. Judgments Invoked 34
7. Acts of Nature 40
8. Mysteries Disclosed 43

III
CHILDREN'S FRIGHTS

∙8. Devil, Demons and Monsters 53

ᐧ IV
ACTS OF THE DEVIL

10. The Devil's Importance 65
11. The Devil Comes for His Own 69
12. The Devil and the Preacher 87
13. Funning the Devil 91
14. Outwitting the Devil 99
15. Sundry Devil Tales 106

- 16. Spirits of Forbidding Places 113
- 17. Magic and Miscellaneous 129

V
PORTENTS AND OMENS

- 18. Death Portents 139

VI
GHOSTS, HA'NTS AND SPECTRES

- 19. Bridges to Eternity 155
- 20. Messages From the Dead 166
- 21. Guardians of the Living 172
- 22. The Dead Boss the Living 187
- 23. Ghost Magic and Controls 196
- 24. Craving Ghosts 203
- 25. Scary Ghosts 214
- 26. Treasure Guardians 223
- 27. Laughing With the Ghosts 234
- 28. There Ain't No Ghosts 242

Notes and Bibliography 245

Index 251

Illustrations

War in Heaven—by Albrecht Duer 15
'You shall go to hell with me tonight!' 22
She saw the image of her Annie in the headstone .. 26
'I reach over and jab him through his hairy coat' .. 31
'Something big and spottedy just a-flopping' 37
A big red whiskered man disembarks with his men 47
The Indian's 'Flying Head' 60
The Kingdom of Darkness—by Nathaniel Crouch 63
Coming at Old Jerry was a black hairy thing 71
The light flared to blinding brilliance 74
The visitor busies himself with hair curlers 76
Grandma beats the Devil off 80
What Aunt Betty saw 96
One Sunday he pulled up a ball of fire 111
He looked into the eyes of a blue-eyed rabbit 114
'My God come quickly!' 119
Sometimes an Imp appears in behalf of the Devil 137
The mist took the form of a woman with a veil .. 146

Old Judge takes his place below master's window 164

The image was 'a light bulb with my father's face.' 168

Annie looks into the face of her mother 174

'He des stan' dere, look at you, look at de baby' .. 178

Evangeline comes back to ha'nt almost every night 181

Here comes Old Master riding by 190

Mose comes and slaps Queenie on the neck 198

The old man comes back for his whiskey 206

All parts of a human body fall 218

He went off crawling frightened half to death 226

Some Glimpses

TIME after time monster children have been born to profane and wicked parents. Not long ago in Newsoms, Virginia, this woman was bad sick, so when her baby was born "it was the natural little devil, had horns on the head." And his pa "jest set around and look at 'im...."

—o—

THE DEVIL was the spitting image of a bear that night when he came for Old Jerry. But Old Jerry was expecting him and had the Bible at his bedside to hold him off.

—o—

NO LESS than one banshee came to North Carolina. Before the Revolution one such spectral lady of the pine barrens haunted the country along the Tar River a little below present Tarboro. She was as hardy as the grizzly human pioneers and a terror when compared with her kind in native Celtic countries.

—o—

AFTER Old Master died his slave girl decided she would marry this no 'count man, and when they stood before the preacher here come Old Master out of the east "in his old surrey all lighted up popping his whip over the heads of four white horses galloping like lightning."

—o—

AFTER Mr. Lenow's first wife died in Rocky Mount he took a second one in Bertie County. And when he died the first one sent their old coach with coachman and attendants after him.

PART I
The Traditional Heritage

1.
Rich and Diverse Traditions

FROM its beginning in 1663 North Carolina has had a rich folk tradition. The first settlers were largely a few planters and their white servants who came southward from Virginia. These servants for the most part were indentures who became free and independent small farmers when their contracted terms of service had been completed. A few Indian servants likewise gained their freedom. Thus it became expedient to introduce Negro slaves to guarantee a continuing labor force.

During the seventeenth century the population was never large, at no time over 5,000. The settlers were scattered about the Albemarle Sound and along its tributary rivers and creeks. Like Virginia, Maryland and colonies to the north, it was a maritime colony; and the waterways invited merchants and seamen from New England.

As the eighteenth century opened John Lawson published a *history* which was to become one of the colony's most important literary works. Virtually all of the information contained in it is a combination of the author's own observations and the country's oral history and traditions. He tells us clearly that these traditions were about as English as those of the Mother Country.

The tales of "many Hobgoblins and Bugbears" were widespread. Nurses and servants told the children "idle Tales of Fairies, and Witches." These, he says, made "such Impression on our tender years, that at Maturity, we carry Pigmies' Souls in Giants' bodies."

The planting of such deep fears made the people "ever after . . . so much deprived of Reason, and unmanned, as never to be Masters of half the Bravery Nature designed for us." (L2, p. 213). *

Two centuries and more after Lawson traditions had a major influence on North Carolina's folk culture. Generation after generation the people responded to new influences until much of the English purity had been lost and a great diversity acquired.

The forces of change began to appear late in the seventeenth century. In 1696 William Randolph said "Pyrates & runaway Servants resort to this place from Virginia . . ." (NCCR, I, 467). The loosely administered Proprietary government permitted growing lawlessness which was climaxed with Blackbeard's piratical forays. The Devil no longer had to retire to the underground to find darkness. He only had to come to wild and shady Carolina. From out of such wildness the *Great Beast* emerged as an awe inspiring reality.

But close behind the demon with forked tail, cloven hoofs, horned head, appropriately called *Old Hairy*, came the itinerant preacher, footwashed from wading many streams and splashes. The Anglican clergyman, sent out by the Society for the Propagation of the Gospel in Foreign Parts, was coolly received by the common people. For one thing, they did not wish

---

A simple reference system has been adopted for this work. Turn to Notes and Bibliography for the key to abbreviations. For example, "L2" stands for Lawson, John, "Lawson's History of North Carolina."

Also, a simple symbol system to designate race of informants has been adopted: (WA) is White American; (BA) Black American; (AI) American Indian; and (J) Juvenile.

to support him by taxation; and, another, this churchman did not use enough fanfare in driving back Old Hairy. It is suspected that a good many rugged characters preferred the excitement of having the itinerant scare the hell out of them.

In 1704 Dr. John Blair, an Anglican minister, lamented that in this colony there were a great many Quakers and also a great many who had no religion. He spoke of his itinerant rivals as men "who have left their lawful employment, and preach and baptize through the country, without any manner of orders from any sect or pretended church." (NCCR, I, 601).

Immediately after defeat the the Tuscarora Indians in 1713, which removed the Indian threat from the frontier, virtually all of the fertile lands of the coastal plains were taken up. Growth in spiritual concern did not equal the growth in population. In 1742 the Reverend John Garcia explained "immorality is arrived to that head among so many, that it requires not only some time but great patience to conqueor it." In his parish "adultery, Incest, Blasphemy, and all kinds of profaneness has got . . . deep root." (NCCR, IV, 604)..

At this time a New England religious revival known as the Great Awakening was preparing men to reshape the religious and folk life of North Carolina. By 1760 the frontier had advanced across the piedmont to the mountains. That year the Reverend James Reed, an Anglican minister of New Bern, observed "there are too many that can hardly be said to be members of any particular christian society, and the great number of dissenters of all denominations come and settle amongst us from New Engd particularly, Anabaptists, Methodists, Quakers and Presbyterians." He found the Anabaptists "obstinate, illiterate & grossly ignorant;" the Methodists, "ignorant, censorious & uncharitable," the Quakers, "Rigid;" and the Presbyterians, "pretty moderate except here & there a bigot or rigid calvanist." (NCCR, VI, 265).

The *Great New England Detour* in folk traditions was being completed. Folk tales and folk beliefs of the seventeenth century were transplanted in North Carolina during the eighteenth. Itinerant preachers—often bearded, ragged, sweat-smelly—came forth wielding a two-edged sword: the threat of instantaneous destruction at the hand of Providence and for those who escaped that, eternal torture of the soul in hell fire. Out of this ferment came vivid imagery of contending spiritual forces, and some of this same imagery survived cheerfully in virtually all parts of the state throughout the nineteenth century. And traces of it may be found in today's folk tradition.

Immediately before the Revolution, in 1773, Josiah Quincy gave the composition of the population. "You see husbandmen, yeomen, and white laborers scattered through the country, instead of herds of negroes and slaves. . . . Property is much more diffused . . . and this may account for some, if not all the differences of character in the inhabitants. . . ." (NCCR, IX, 612)

James Davis' press, established a few years earlier at New Bern, had little influence on the lives of many of the people. News continued to be circulated by word of mouth. The folk tale was an immensely popular form of entertainment. Travelers who were good story tellers and bearers of news were welcome in most homes.

It seemed to matter little that some of the religious leaders were almost as unlettered as their listeners. Preachers who were good story tellers were among the more popular. When they began to mesmerize their audiences the religious folk tale began to burst into flower.

Anglican clergymen found the New Lights reprehensible. The Reverend Mr. Reed explained that they were accustomed to "crying-out,. . .falling down in fits, . . . awakening in extacies, and impulses, visions and revelations." (P4, p. 383).

One Mr. Woodman reported in 1766 that this extremely Arminian sect had penetrated the whole back country across North Carolina into South Carolina.

"Some of them lately killed a traveling Person and cut him into atoms singing Hymns making processions and Prayers and offering up this inhuman sacrifice to the Deity as an acceptable oblation." One of their leaders was hanged for the murder and one of their teachers pretended to work miracles and declared that he had the power "equal with Christ and that God had given him authority even to raise the dead." (NCCR, VII, 286-287).

During the Revolution, in part because of camp life, the old vices returned. Preachers became alarmed over the prevalence of gaming, card-playing, heavy drinking and profanity. (J9, p. 27).

New preachers joined in an evangelical movement continuing the pace set by those inspired by the Great Awakening. They built up a great surge of emotionalism, stirring the people's superstitious fear of the Devil and frightening them into salvation. Often the meetings were climaxed by people seeing visions, entering into trances and talking in tongues.

It had been customary for the people to attribute things that they could not understand to the work of either God or the Devil. God was an active overseer of the behavior of man and acted through Providence. In Northampton County the assembly was profoundly effected when the Rev. John Easter prayed that rain which had begun to fall be delayed until after services and then continue as the rain was needed, "and it happened according to his petition." (J9, p. 25).

In 1901, in Orange County ". . .many were struck down, or thrown into a state of helplessness if not insensibly . . . Bating (sic) the miraculous attestations from Heaven, such as cloven tongues like fire and the power of speaking different languages . . ." (J9, p. 30).

The revival movement increased in momentum reaching its climax about 1804. Hideous representations of the Devil, vivid descriptions of future torment, and awful denunciations of God's wrath coming from the pulpit (J9, p. 43) made a lasting impression on the public mind.

Meanwhile the telling of folk tales was immensely popular. Late in the eighteenth century people coming down to the Roanoke River in Martin County "were very superstitions, and could tell marvelous tales of witches, ghosts, and apparitions." (R3, 30-31).

Rev. Brantley York, born in 1805, stated that in Randolph County where he spent his boyhood people "believed in Witchcraft, Ghost-seeing, haunted houses and fortune telling. When neighbors visited "the most prominent topic of conversation was relating some remarkable witch tales, ghost stories and conjurations of various kinds; and so interesting was these stories that the conversation often continued until a very late hour at night." (Y2, p. 8f).

Dr. J. B. Jeter, born in 1802, says that in Bedford County, Virginia: "Story-telling was one of the common amusements of the times; and these stories usually related to witches, hags, giants, prophetic dreams, ghosts and the like." The Jack-o'-lantern, graveyards, ghosts and the like were dreaded. (H4, p. 36f).

War in Heaven—by Albrecht Duer.

PART II
Acts of Providence

2.
The Workings of Providence

THE Christian emigrant brought with him to the New World a firm belief in Providence. And in seventeenth century, says Richard Dorson, eminent folklorist, this meant that "every event on earth and movement in the heavens could be directly caused by God, if he so willed. Or if he preferred, God could work his will through ordinary means."

The firm believer looked for God's message in the remarkable happening or strange movement in the heavens. The meanig of some events was unmistakable, but others required close scrutiny and examination to determine what God had in mind.

God's wrath "struck the idolatrous, the blasphemers, the heathen, the transgressors of his law and the followers of Satan with sure and obvious judgments." On the other hand, "his goodness saved the faithful from the most perilous plight, by holy deliverances and preservations." (D5, p. 123).

Midway and at the conclusion of the eighteenth century the Great Awakening and the Great Revival created new religious awareness and thus gave emphasis to the belief in Providence. This led to the enrichment of the folk tradition. To this time one may find many stories of providential happenings quite similar to those recorded in the seventeenth century. Signs, omens, and portents appear in many ways. Monster children are sent as warning to ungodly parents; blasphemers are driven raving mad or destroyed; judgment is suspended in a crime of passion; brimstone-tipped lightning bolts are hurled from the sky; things are rearranged according to God's intent by storms, floods, tornadoes and earthquakes; and attempts to explore the moon and other celestial bodies are forbidden.

3.

Warnings

Monster Children

For about three centuries divine Providence has pointed an accusing finger at wicked American parents, causing them to have monster children.

That such belief was firmly rooted during the first half of the seventeenth century is evident in the writings of John Winthrop, governor of the Massachusetts colony.

About one-half of a century before the Salem witch trials a monster daughter was born to a woman who had been branded as a heretic. The child of Satan "had a face but no head, and the ears stood upon the shoulders and like an ape's; it had no forehead, but over the eyes four horns, hard and sharp (two of them were above one inch long, the other two shorter), the eyes standing out, and the mouth also; the nose hooked upward; and all over the breast and back full of sharp pricks and scales, like a thornback; and the navel and all the belly, with the distinction of the sex, were where the back should be, and the back and hips before, where the belly should have been; behind, between the shoulders, it had two mouths, and in each of them a piece of red flesh sticking out; it had no arms and legs as other children, but instead of toes it had on each foot three claws like a young fowl with sharp talons."

Winthrop supposed that God had sent the child as a warning to the parents as he had done in several other instances of which he himself had knowledge. (W12).

The Nash County Monster (WA)

A similar line of thought appears to have been taken by itinerant ministers and planted in frontier communities southward from New England through North Carolina. That monster stories were effective in hustling sinners into salvation is self-evident. For these were being told by both white and black preachers only a few years ago.

One story comes from one Bruce Andrews who moved from Cumberland County to Bladen County about 1918. For several years he tilled a small farm on Black River, Lake Creek Township. Often Andrews visited his neighbors and sat with them late at night telling tales about witches, ghosts and extraordinary events.

Andrews said that while living in Cumberland County he had attended a revival meeting and heard a high spirited evangelist tell of the birth of a monster child in nearby Nash County.

The father was notorious for his wickedness. He partook of each and every vice that the Devil had conjured. The result of heavy drinking was a wife and several children, hungry and ragged, crowded into a hovel open to cold in winter and deluged by rain. Entirely without honor and the fear of God, he entertained lewd women and blasphemed.

Then another child was born, and this one was a monster, horrible to view. For some time no one was permitted to see the child other than the midwife, and the mother sent her home as soon as she could return to her duties. But the secret couldn't be kept. It was told about the neighborhood that the infant's face was badly deformed and that two horns about three inches long projected from the top of his head.

Some of the neighbors said that the child was sent as a warning to the father. He should forsake his wickedness. Soon afterwards a revival was held in the community, and the father was persuaded to attend the services. Fear of God's wrath weighed upon him, and he begged forgiveness for his sins and found salvation. Happy to be out of the clutches of the Devil he became very devout. People remarked that now he was as godly as he had been ungodly.

This father became a pillar of the church and a credit to his community. Thereafter he wore a smile, even in the face of adversity. Meanwhile his monster child underwent a marvelous change. The horns disappeared from his head, and his face became a wonder of beauty. When the son grew to manhood he became a prominent attorney and was elected to the state legislature. (A2).

—*Bruce Andrews.*

The Hertford County Monster (WA)

Once an offending parent had been warned and continued unrepentant he or she invited the terrible wrath of Providence. One such father was duly punished in a folk story as related by Mrs. Judy Godwin Mizelle, a native of Ahoskie, Hertford County, North Carolina:

This handsome man and woman had been married for years. And the husband told his wife, "We don't want to have any children. I want all your love." But his wife got pregnant anyway and he didn't like it. In fact he hated it. He got angry and violent. He took it out on his wife. He cursed her and he cursed everything; he was so mad. And one day when he came home from work and found her knitting some clothes for their expected baby he cursed her and beat her; and he told her that he wasn't going to have anything to do with the baby when it came. Dam' it.

His wife got upset and nervous, so upset that she started reading the Bible to find some comfort. But one day her husband came home and saw her reading it. That made him mad, so mad that he scolded: "Everything you want to do since you've been carrying that baby is to read that damn book." And he snatched the Bible out of her hands and threw it into the fire. "Dam' that youngan to hell. . . .

His wife got so upset that she went into labor right then. He wouldn't help her; he wouldn't even call anybody to help. So the baby was born early and she had to do it all without any help. And when it was born it was a monster, a regular little monster. It looked like the Devil. It had two little horns on its head, and had fangy teeth and red eyes that sparkled flashes of fire.

That woman saw it and was horrified. She broke down crying. She told her husband he was to blame; the baby had been sent as a warning that he had better repent or be damned. But the father of the child just cursed something awful; he fumed and ranted worse that he had ever done since they were married.

A few nights after that, like his old wicked self, he

'You shall go to hell with me tonight!'

was just a-cursing. It was some kind of bad, something awful. And his wife was weeping, and the tears were streaming down her face when the little baby sits up in his crib, and he points a finger straight at his father and he says, as grown up as you ever did see, and he says to his father, "Man of Satan," and waits until he looks real hard with steely eyes, "you shall go to hell with me tonight!"

Then that little devil jumps right out of his crib into the roaring fire they had burning in the fireplace. He then pointed at the man . . . his father . . . His father screamed a scream of the damned . . . like the Devil himself had him. His little son, that little devil, carried him right away with him . . . into the raging fire of hell and damnation, forever. (M7)
—Judy Godwin (Mrs. Ernest) Mizelle.

The Monster of Gums (BA)

A second folk monster story comes from a black Virginia informant, Susie Brooks, who lives near Newsoms a few miles north of the line with North Carolina. The following taped report also tells of the fate of an unrepentant father:

This baby was born down in Gums, other side of Newsoms down dere. This family lived in Gums and this baby was borned.

This woman, her husband so mean that every time he'd git out, go out of his house, he sweep his yard so he can tell if anybody walks back in that yard that had tracks.

She was sick, Lawd, that woman was sick, and so last of that week this woman's baby was born. So when the baby was born the baby was born like the Devil, had horns on his head.

You see her old man had told his wife, said, "I'd

'ruther see de Devil in this house than see you. So when the baby was born it was born the Devil. So when the baby was born, o-o-o-o-up, it was the natural little devil, had little horns sticking on the head.

The third day the baby looked at his mother and say, "Mother, I'm going to leave you now," and sailed out of the bed and sailed into the fire."

And this was true. This was down in Gums, Virginia.

You know, she told that. I know that woman wouldn't have told that lie.

When the husband saw that child he didn't say nothing. He jest set around and looked at 'im, and then thought about what he had said.

It scared him to death. But he still was mean and all, like the Devil himself.

So finally the old man went to the log woods, I'll never forget that; and the old man went into the log woods and a tree fell on him and killed him.

The Lord did that, the Lord did it. He punish. If you don't do right, better look out for the Lord.

Don't have to look out after the Devil. He happy, you know he happy. (B17).

—*Susie Brooks.*

4.
Messages

The Image in the Tombstone (WA)

Sometimes prayers of the worthy were answered in a variety of ways, some very strangely as revealed in a story heard in Bladen County, North Carolina:

Some fifty years ago the Reverend Daniel Savant came to the Rowan Creek community of Bladen County to hold revival services at the local church.

Savant was a powerful speaker, such a force that after a night or two all seats were taken, chairs crowded the aisle, and people listened through the open door and windows to the words and wisdom of the good man.

As the minister spoke attentive uplifted faces were caught up in the yellow glow of the kerosene lamps hanging from the unpainted tongued and grooved wooden walls. Between his pauses such was the stillness that one may have heard a pin drop upon the floor.

And one of those listeners of a half-century ago recalls one of the Reverend Savant's stories of Christian experiences:

Years before that, how many was not disclosed, the death angel had visited the home of a Scotch-Irish family living near Fair Bluff in Columbus County, and taken their most prized possession. Family members, relatives, neighbors and friends were grieved at the death of a good and beautiful girl, whose name perhaps was Annie. People couldn't put their grief

She saw the image of her Annie in the headstone.

into words, but the minister likened her to a spring flower which had been crushed asunder.

Although Annie had found her faith at an early age she suffered with delirium and high fevers; and then death came hard. This worried her mother; why had she suffered so much? why so innocent an one? So in her prayers she would ask God for a sign to let her know if her little darling girl had gone to paradise.

Not long after Annie's death the family placed a headstone at her grave in the family cemetery This was of beautiful white marble, and the stone cutter had fashioned a beautiful white angel with open wings for its top, giving praise to God.

Annie's mother came often to the burial plot and said prayers at Annie's graveside. One day she noticed that a faint image had appeared in the headstone. At first she could not make out what it was. So each day she came, and each time the image became more and more distinct.

Then one day she knew. Her prayers had been answered, for here in front of her was the image of Annie in the tombstone, and upon her shoulders was a pair of open wings like those of the marble angel above.

She fell down on her knees and praised God. (J12).
—*Nolon Johnson.*

A Message From a Mother (WA)

The Bullhead community of Greene County, North Carolina, is about ten miles northwest of the county seat town of Snow Hill and near the Wilson County line. It's beautiful farm country, rolling gently as it follows the southwestern bank of Contentnea Creek. It seems symbolic. The endless fertile farms regenerate green life as unfailingly as the coming of each spring.

So it has done since the early settlers cleared back the forests. Likewise, until a few years ago old families were regenerated with each new generation while the family cemetery upon the slope of a hill grew upon the call for each worn and weary life.

Few of the old families still remain. And that is true of our particular one. But the family cemetery, overgrown with vines and shrubs, stands in the middle of the field. So hidden is a tomb which pays tribute to a mother of a long time ago.

It is evident that this mother lived before the advent of modern medicine, for she joined the large number of mothers who died in childbirth.

This particular one was young and loved by her husband, relatives and friends. Her child also died in their struggle for life.

Grief for her was not only bitter; it was long lasting, day after day, week after week, month after month, year after year. The new headstone in her memory seemed to add to their grief.

One day the distraught husband visited his wife's grave. He was astonished to see dark lines rambling about the white, he had thought perfect, marble. He called others. Then all were amazed at what they saw.

In the stone was the image of a mother smiling down at an infant which she held in her arms.

The message was clear. "Mother and child are in a happy state."

—*Anonymous.*

The Gun in the Tombstone

Should one look very closely one might make out the image of a shotgun in a headstone in the Old Mt. Hermon Church cemetery in Wake County, North Carolina.

In 1928 one Roy Chopplin of the neighborhood connected this image with the story of one Mr. Jackson whom the marker commemorates.

Jackson was a hot tempered man, Chopplin recalled. One day he was angered over a minor matter, and this led to a fury that bordered on insanity. He took down his shotgun, shot his wife and several children to death and then killed himself.

People had begun to forget Jackson and his terrible deed when a strange occurence refreshed their memories. A dark figure began to appear in his headstone. At first it was not clear, but after some time it became quite distinct. It was an image of a shotgun. Some said it was like Jackson's murder weapon. (C3).

5.
Judgments Suspended

Saved From the Gallows (WA)

"Yessir," said Levi while leaning against his plow handles resting his mule from plowing our garden, "yessir, I believes that sometimes the Lord looks after us and keeps us out of trouble when he sees that we will do better another time.

"I wouldn't be here now.... I would be rotting in my grave ... they would have put a rope around my neck if HE hadn't stepped in and helped me one time when I was young and hot headed."

Levi began telling me how I should hurry up and get my Irish potatoes in the ground while it was still the dark of the moon and how if I waited too long it would be *bug days* and the bugs would eat them up. But I was more interested in how Levi had escaped the hangman.

"I've heard of people getting rain by sincere prayer, but how did the Lord save you, Levi?"

"Dat was about fifty years ago, and I was living down in Edgecombe County (North Carolina) between Rocky Mount and Tarboro, and I was working for Mr. Gurganus on his farm.

"Two or three miles from there was this yaller gal . . . some kind of purty . . . and I got to going to her house. I got so het up that I beg her to marry me, but she stand me off . . . say she got to have time to make up her mind.

She was my gal, I thinks, but one night when I goes over to sit she won't let me in her house. I begs and she says, 'I got a headache, but I be better by tomorrow night.' I gits the feeling she is trying to hide something from me, and I waits a time and then goes around and looks in the window. What I sees makes me as mad as a bull cow. There is that gal all tied up with that black boy Sammy from over at Mr. Jim Snook's farm.

"I is ready to break in dere and beat them both up, but I figures that be too good for that black nigger. So I pokes on home, cussing, getting madder. I gets out my butcher knife, sharpens it to cut to kill. Then I goes back to where Sammy got to climb over the rail fence back of Mr. Snook's field. I waits and I waits until the moon goes down and it gits so dark you can't see much of nothing.

"Along about eleven or twelve o'clock I hears something coming out of the woods and walking down the

'I reach over and jab him through his huiry coat.'

path. It like he is stumbling along drunk, and I gits my butcher knife ready, I going to cut that nigger's heart out.

"He come up to the fence, and I reach over and grab him by the neck, pull him over and jab him through his hairy coat one time, two time, three time . . . until he falls down dead.

"Den I gets scared, I have killed a man, they going to hang me down in Tarboro fer certain. So I runs to my boss' house and gets him out of bed. 'Mr. Gurganus, you got to help me, I done killed Black Sammy.

" 'We go see before we call the law,' say my boss. He gets his lantern, and we goes down there. He goes ahead with the lantern, and I tells him just where it is.

" 'Bless my hide, Levi, don't you know what you have done?' He sets his lantern down and turns the thing over. 'They ain't going to hang you. They is going to give you a medal or something. You've killed that old bear that has been raiding our corn fields.'

"That scared me worse than ever . . . when I sees I been in the arms of that bear. I breaks out in a sweat until I is wet all over. I makes Mr. Gurganus let me walk out ahead and walk with me to my cabin. . . . I is so upsot.

"I got down and got saved the next chance I gets. I figures the Lord saved me from hanging this time, but he might not do it again.

"I never go see that yaller gal again. I puts her off when she asks me why I stays away. I figures if she wants Sammy she can have Sammy.

"See, I'm up in my seventies now, and I ain't never been in no real bad trouble. That was God's work. He know'd I was going to git right." (W10).

—*Clayton Wiggins.*

Spared From Lightning

After five strikes a Shenandoah National Park ranger is certain that he will not be hit by lightning again. He explained that he was advised in a dream that God is sparing him "for some good purpose."

Previous dreams, he said, had warned him of his oncoming troubles. And after being hit four times he became convinced that some supernatural force was out to get him. In July 1972 there was this dream, and on August 7 he was hit his fifth time. When he saw a storm gathering he tried to get out of its path. And when he thought he had outrun it he pulled into the Eaton Hollow area. He had barely stepped from his truck when the lightning bolt "struck me right on the head, set my hair on fire, traveled down my left leg, knocking off my shoe but not untying the lace." He was knocked about ten feet and the blow felt like that from a heavyweight.

Sullivan doused his burning hair with a bucket of water and received treatment for second degree burns in a Waynesville, Virginia, hospital.

He had been listed in the Guiness Book of World Records as the "only living man to be struck by lightning four times." Now they are having to up that to five times.

He lost a toenail from his first strike in 1942. In 1969 he was knocked unconcious; and in 1970 his hair was burned off . . . all while working for the park service.

—*The Associated Press.*

6.
Judgments Invoked

Punished for Blasphemy

During the seventeenth century a certain way to invite punishment at the hands of Providence was to express contempt for God through blasphemy. Like witchcrafts and murder, it was regarded as a cardinal crime by the courts, a crime instigated directly by the Devil.

In some instances blasphemy warranted immediate punishment, but at other times the offender awaited trial before the *Seat of Judgment*. Clergymen cited varous instances of the crime and its punishment.

In 1633, writes the Reverend John Eliot, an ungodly man in the heat of passion would "wish himself in hell" and use desperate words. His wish was not long in being answered. He and a companion were drowned when trapped on an oyster bank by a rising tide. (E2, p. 242).

A Jesuit missionary, in 1642, writes of a man who in sacrilegious playfulness packed his pipe with prayer beads. Soon afterwards he went swimming and was attacked by a large fish which bit away a large portion of his thigh. While suffering great pain he was hurried away from the land of the living. (N1; D5, pp. 138-139).

A seaman, writes John Winthrop, insisted on lighting a pipe of tobacco aboard a ship which was well stocked with powder. He would have it, he said, "if the Devil would carry him away quick." The Devil got him quickly; a barrel of powder caught fire and blasted him and several of his unfortunate companions into eternity. (W14, I, p. 82).

To this time in North Carolina folk tales disclose that blasphemy may invoke immediate punishment at the hand of Providence.

Thunderbolt Slays Blasphemer (BA)

"I started to carry one of them things home, but I decided not to; I didn't want it in the house during a storm." Then seventy-three-year-old Edward Beverly of Hertford County, North Carolina, explained, "Peoples say it will draw lightning."

Edward's Indian grandmother Celia Mitchell, born and raised in Bertie County's Indian Woods, told him about the *thunderbolt*. That was soon after opening of the twentieth century as she rested out her concluding years at the home of his parents in the Oak Villa community near the town of Winton.

The thunderbolt is made of brimstone, the fuel for hell fire, Grandmother Celia asserted. Sometimes the Lord tips lightning with it and tosses it to earth to warn or strike down sinners.

Grandmother Celia knew of several people who had so suffered from God's wrath. His message was unmistakable. Wherever the bolt struck the earth was poisoned; all vegetation refused to grow in a large circle about the spot.

As a proper example, Grandmother Celia told of the awful fate of one John Brown, a wicked old man who lived in Indian Woods when she was a girl. He was a woodsman, working mostly as a turpentine scraper and a tar maker. Some folks said he was in league with the Devil, practiced some conjure, and he did not deny it. Instead, one might hear him cry in rage against his hard work and poor living. He owed God nothing for his pittance of beans, ground corn and pickled pork; but all knew that he was ever in debt for his brandy and could have afforded better fare had he left off drinking.

One day Old John and another man were firing a newly laid tar kiln when a severe electrical storm boiled from beneath the horizon and swept over them. Seeing that their new fire might be drenched with torrents of rain, Old John flew into a rage. He balled up his fist, shook it at the boiling and rumbling yellow cloud and shouted, "I dare you to strike me!"

Instantly there came a blinding flash and a deafening crash. The blasphemer's body lay prostrate . . . lifeless . . . charred black . . . in smouldering rags.

Old John's companion, shaken and stunned, saw a white hot steam reeking with the stench of sulphur rise in a circle about Old John's body.

When men of the neighborhood removed Old John's body for burial they found a thunderbolt, shaped like an Indian arrowhead, beneath it. The thunderbolt was still quivering. "It shook," declared Grandmother Celia, "just like rattlesnake rattles." (B10).

—*Edward Beverly.*

The Aunt Who Blasphemed (BA)

My father told me about this woman who was mean and how her meaness got her into trouble, said eleven-year-old Tony Wiggins of Como, Hertford County, North Carolina. One hot day she was out there in the field with the other folks chopping peanuts (hoeing out the grass). The wind wasn't blowing and

'Something big and spottedy just a-flopping'

everybody got hot. When this woman got hot she got mad and took to cursing. That just made her madder, and she cursed some awful. She cursed the heat, she cursed the peanuts, and she cursed everything she could think of.

And after awhile she cursed God for sending so much heat. Everybody heard her, and she shocked all of them so that they let up hoeing and looked at her. Anybody with any sense at all know it is mighty dangerous.

"Look!" said my daddy, and everybody looked up. They see something big and spottedy just a-flopping and a-coming down out of the air. They see it doesn't have a head; and then it disappears.

Everybody is scared, but this woman is so scared that she lits out for the house as fast as she can run. When she gets to the door they hear her scream like she is dying.

They run to see what is the matter, and she say when she opened the door that spottedy thing is standing right in front of her. They look all over the house but can't find it.

Everybody but this woman go back to chopping. Soon they hear her scream again, and they run back to the house.

But they can't find her in the house. They look out back of the hog pen, and they don't find her. They go down in the thicket beside the swamp, and they don't find her. And they go to this brier patch back of the field. There she is in the briers. And is lying down in there, torn up by the briers. And there is a pitchfork sticking through her breast.

They all say that spottedy thing must have killed her for cursing the Lord. (W12).

—*Tony Wiggins.*

The Picture Taker (BA)

One Sunday a few years ago a girl brought her new camera to church, and before the preaching she was taking pictures of all her friends.

But when she pointed her camera at one boy he said to her, "Don't you take my picture!" and he meant it. He sounded like he meant it.

That made the girl angry, and she was touched with evil. She pointed her camera at the sky and she said, "Well then, I'll take a picture of that SOB up yonder." And the folks, a lot of them, heard the camera shutter. They were shocked; they were afraid.

When the girl got her pictures back from the picture house all of them were good and clear, even the one she took of the sky. But this one frightened her; in it was the face of Jesus Christ. She got rid of that picture, gave it to a girl friend.

But that did her no good; she couldn't get what she had done out of her mind. She was scared, and she worried about it; she worried herself right out of her mind. They had to take her away to the crazy house.

It wasn't long before folks back home heard that the girl had died and that she had died raving mad. (M10).

—*Dallas Moore.*

7.
Acts of Nature

The Church Called 'Providence'

There are numerous churches of various faiths called Providence, but there is one in North Carolina which undoubtedly is appropriately named.

This is Providence Methodist Church in the quiet Hyde County fishing village of Swan Quarter, made county seat in 1836. According to local tradition it was named for the beautiful white swan which winters nearby in lush grassy feeding grounds bordering the Pamlico Sound. (S3, II, p. 905). But it is more likely that the village was named for Samuel F. Swan, an early owner of the site. (P15, p. 484).

Midway the 1870's a handful of local Methodists got together and made plans to erect a meeting house. Most were of such modest means that they contributed labor and materials rather than cash. By 1876 they were ready to build.

A site committee agreed on one in the heart of the village and which had a distant view of Swan Quarter Bay. But the rich landowner had other plans for the lot and declined to sell. So the less desirable lot was purchased.

A brick foundation was laid, and the frame building slowly took shape. As soon as it had a roof, floor and unfinished walls members proudly assembled for meetings.

In mid-September disaster seemed to strike; but a guiding force changed this into a great good.

On the night of the sixteenth, which had been set for the dedication, a storm broke. Gale winds swept across Swan Quarter Bay and bore down upon the town. The winds howled through the night, and by morning waters of the bay flooded the streets. At last the winds abated but the waters continued to rise.

Then a strange thing happened. The new church shuddered and floated from its brick foundation. Now the waters began to recede, and the church floated down the street riding free of fences, trees and other obstructions until it came to a general store. A corner lodged against this building and the churning waters from an intersection spun it across a drainage canal where it lodged against some small trees and settled with the receding waters. It came to rest in the middle of the lot which the rich man had refused to sell.

This man immediately volunteered to donate the lot and lent building jacks for building a new foundation. And he was at the courthouse early next morning to deed the property to the Methodists.

The story of the little church's quest for a home was widely circulated. Many people came for its first services, so many that large numbers had to listen from the grounds.

The membership was unanimous in choice of a name for their church . . . Providence.

The lot donor remarked, "I had plans for that land, but it appears that God had His too!" (S3, II, p. 906).

(After a number of years the church membership outgrew its original building. A new brick building was erected on the site. For a time the old building was used as a barn, but then it was returned to the grounds and remodeled for a Sunday school department. (W7, pp. 100-105).

Man Can't Go to the Moon (BA)

"Now if you want to know the foundation of things, you go where it is started at. The starting point is these older people." And they in their traditional wisdom have been her chief guidance, says Maggie Artis of Southampton County, Virginia.

"Granpa and them used to tell by signs . . . fish won't bite on a new moon, but they will bite on the waste of the moon. . . .

"I don't believe man can go to the moon without upsetting God's elements.

"You know we had a flood over here in Courtland in October . . . a lot of people come to see all that water . . . .

"People talking about before this flood them astronauts going to the moon. One lady say, 'Look like every time they go up yonder to the moon something happen.'

"I say, 'Lady, you know why?' I say, 'God put man down here on earth, and if he can't handle what's down here on earth, how he going to handle where God ain't put him.'

" 'Now, down here (on earth) with this water man can't move this water!'

"They say, 'No!'

"I say, 'We can move this water as good as we can go to God's moon. 'Tis out of man's reach.'

"Here the other week people went to the moon, and they had a earthquake (in Central America) and 'stroyed I don't know how many people.

"God is displeased with man doing things he didn't ask him to do." (A5).

—*Maggie Artis.*

.8

Mysteries Disclosed

Raleigh's Spectre Ship

"I cannot forbear inserting here a pleasant story that passes for an uncontested truth among the inhabitants of this place (Carolina): which is, that the ship which brought the first colonies does often appear among them, under sail, in a pleasant posture, which they call Sir Walter Raleigh's ship. And the truth of this has been affirmed to me by men of the best credit in the country." So writes John Lawson in 1709. (L2, p. 62).

Raleigh's spectre ship was but one of several which had appeared in the New World during the seventeenth and eighteenth centuries.

The early sightings come from the pens of some of the more prominent chroniclers of events.

The great loss of small, frail wooden sailing ships together with lives of mariners and passengers upon the stormy Atlantic created a source of both grief to kinsmen and friends and of concern to virtually all of the colonists.

The Spectre of New Haven

The spectre at New Haven is an example. In 1647, Cotton Mather quotes the Reverend James Pierpont as saying, a ship richly laden with goods and carrying many prominent passengers, put out from the port for England. And the following year when no word came from her many a heart grew heavy. The people turned to public and private prayer and begged the Lord to let them hear "what he had done with their dear friends."

The Lord's reply came upon a June evening when a great thunderstorm arose out of the northwest. Serenity permeated the skies after the storm, and "about an hour before sunset a ship like the dimension" of the lost one, "with her canvas and colors abroad . . . appeared in the air coming up from our harbor's mouth," sailing against the wind. Thus she sailed as if propelled by a fresh gale for half an hour.

"Many were drwan to behold this great work of God" as the apparition approached to within about a stone's throw of some. Then there was re-enacted the manner of her fate: "her maintop seemed to be blown off, but left hanging in the shrouds; then the mizzentop; then all her masting seemed blown away by the board. Quickly after the hulk brought into a career, she overset, and so vanished into a smoky cloud. . . ." (M2, I, pp. 83-84).

The Spectre at Lynn

Following a thunderstorm mid-winter 1682, writes Noadiah Russell, several inhabitants of Lynn witnessed two strange apparitions. First there came a strange black cloud and after that there appeared an armed man with legs straddling and having a pike drawn across his breast.

After many had seen this apparition the man vanished and in his stead "appeared a spacious ship seeming under sail though she kept the same station." Those who viewed the phantom ship said it was "to their imagination the handsomest of ever they saw—with a lofty stem . . . the hull black, the sails bright. A long and resplendent streamer came from the top of the mast."

After some time it disappeared leaving the sky clear. (R5, pp. 53-54).

—o—

Lawson suggests no providential message in his report on Raleigh's phantom ship. But as the seventeenth century drew to a close the settlements in Carolina were confined almost entirely to the country about the Albemarle Sound. Several "substantial planters from Virginia and other Plantations" had established plantations upon the banks of the several large rivers that were tributary to this sound.

These circumstances seem to suggest that certain of the inhabitants regarded the spectre ship appearing among them as an act of Providence, the ship sailing westward of Roanoke Island, and thus bearing the lost colonists inland.

Blackbeard's Ship

Many years later Edward Teach, the pirate Blackbeard, became a legendary figure, and people who lived upon the Albemarle Sound and its tributaries began seeing a new phantom ship upon the same waters which Raleigh's ship had sailed. It was known as Blackbeard's ship.

The pirate's phantom marked a new trend in the thinking. It was witchy rather than providential. It was seen only on moonlights and bore a curse. The sight of it was a portent of disaster for both the viewer and persons dear to him. (D4).

Meanwhile the pirate's phantom ship was being reported upon the Pamlico Sound near Ocracoke and at several places upon the Pamlico River.

One Bath legend holds that once each one hundred years Blackbeard must return to renew his pact with the Devil to guard his treasure. Mrs. Junius C. Fulford of Pamlico Beach explains, "A century will do away with a ghost," which she says had been left with the chest. (F6). At Bath, it is said, Blackbeard sails his *Queen Anne's Revenge* to the waters off Plum Point and re-enacts the burial of his largest treasure. (W6).

Two Bath residents, Albert Woodard and Ken Totterton, were said to have witnessed Blackbeard's return in 1918. It was mid-summer and the two men were setting their gill nets in Teach's Gut not far from the juncture of Plum Point Bay with the Pamlico River. This particular afternoon they took along some friends for a fish fry.

Woodard and Totterton began frying their fish upon the beach about twilight when one looked out across the Pamlico River and remarked that a pretty schooner was on her way to Washington. Sailing ships were accustomed to hauling grain from this Beaufort County town to northern ports, and appearance of the ship attracted only passing interest.

But soon it was observed that the ship was moving at a very fast speed, faster than anyone thought that a four-master could travel. Then she took an unusual turn, a sharp tack that took her up Bath Creek. She stopped off Teach's Point, and the men on shore heard the sounds of falling tackle and the scraping of chains, and they saw the sails furling.

A big red whiskered man disembarks with his men.

One of the party wondered: How had the ship sailed, without tacking, directly into the brisk northwest wind that was blowing? The men passed that off as a quirk of the wind which sometimes was known to blow from several directions upon gathering of summer storms.

The fishermen busied themselves with gathering firewood and building up the fire. Then Totterton looked out towards the ship and said, "Looks like we're going to have company." A ship's boat was approaching them.

"What in the heavens do you suppose they want?" Woodard asked.

"Search me!" came Totterton's reply.

Once the boat had beached a large red whiskered man got out, and he was followed by six or eight other men. Staring straight ahead and without uttering a word they dragged their boat across the beach through the fishermen's fire and proceeded into the nearby woods.

Soon after the party had disappeared there came voices from the Point. They were confused voices which seemed to rise with anger. Then there came a sharp bark like the firing of a pistol. Instantly the Bay was engulfed in a flaming red light which quickly burned out. The ship was gone, and a grey fog crept over the water where she had been moored.

Woodard, Totterton and their guests, shaken and unbelieving, hurried into town. When their story had been made known some of the older Bath residents recalled that old people of their youth had said that a strange ship appeared in Teach's Gut in 1818, just one-hunded years after Blackbeard lost his life to Maynard at Ocracoke. (W6).

—*Ronald Webster.*

Ship of the Palatines

The phantom *Ship of the Palatines*, driven by Providence, was being sighted off Carolina shores during the first half of the nineteenth century.

The ship's tradition apparently was an outgrowth of a "disastrous and stormy voyage" in 1710 of about one hundred families of German Palatines from England to settle upon Baron De Graffenried's grant at and near present New Bern. About one-half of the emigrants died during thirteen weeks at sea, as the ships entered the James River one was plundered by a French privateer. (L5, pp. 51-52).

The legend appeared in the September 23, 1842, *Carolina Watchman* of Salisbury as a reprint from *The Magnolia; or Southern Appalachian, a Literary Magazine and Monthly Review*, of Charleston, South Carolina. (P11, VI, pp. 23-26). It was stated that according to recent sworn testimonies of credible persons that "at a certain period in every year, a luminous object, having the exact appearance of a ship on fire, appears upon the coast." It had been seen to sail along "with incredible rapidity" as a fiercely burning phantom until out of sight. It then reappeared at its former station and pursued its former route. Thus the ship continued throughout one particular night of the year.

Seeking to explain the phenomenon, it was observed that during the reign of George I a ship was fitted for German Palatines at public expense for transportation to the New World. These emigrants, unlike many of their poor brethren, had gold and valuables, like vessels of silver and fine goods, which they took pains to conceal. After a long and difficult voyage beset with headwinds and sickness the emigrants made the coast of North Carolina. As the ship neared the shore the Palatines began to prepare their baggage for unloading. Either by accident or by some imprudent word the ship's greedy captain learned of their treasures.

"The discovery awakened the devil in his heart," and he signaled his mate of his piratical intent. The passengers were informed that it would be impossible to land them until the next day. The Palatines returned their valuables to the interior of the ship. Most of them took to their hammocks, but a few of their men remained on deck and watched as night swallowed the distant shoreline.

Meanwhile the captain gathered with members of his crew and plotted the murder of the Palatines. Upon a signal each Palatine on deck was struck down. Then below went the murderers, from berth to berth, killing all the Palatines—men, women and children.

Then the murderers grouped around "the treasures which had damned their hearts into the worst hell of covetousness and crime." They divided their spoils and set the ship on fire to conceal their crime. As they pulled for shore in longboats they gazed upon a ship on fire that would not burn. Although the flames "rose triumphantly in air, rushing from stem to stern, from keel to bulwark, from deck to the highest point on the towering mast" the ship was not consumed.

Yet the fire seemed to rage throughout the night as the ship sped on with the wind, passed out of sight only to reappear at her former station and to follow her former course. At dawn the ship was as intact as before the fire was set. It had become, it would seem, the object of "some powerful spell." The same phenomenon reappeared the second night; and the murderers, gravely alarmed, fled from the shore and "buried themselves in the vast interior."

The criminals went free; they and their descendants enjoyed their rich spoils. When the legend was printed in 1842 the phantom ship had been appearing for more than one hundred years, and it was supposed that it would continue to reappear one night each year until "the last descendants of the bloody crew" had paid the "requisite retribution" as required by "ever-avenging Providence." (P11, VII, pp. 23-26).

PART III
Children's Frights

9

Devil, Demons and Monsters

Devil Follows Frontier Westward

The Devil—usually in some monstrous and frightful form—long has been used as a tool to correct and direct children.

And when Carolina was not quite half a century old John Lawson, a recorder of her early folk tradition, observed that tales of hobgoblins and bugbears so impressed the tender ones that fear journeyed with them into their adult lives.

As the settlers moved westward from the coastal swamp and river borders onto the piedmont hills and into the mountain valleys and others pressed up the river valleys out of South Carolina and plod down the valleys out of Virginia the same Old World spirits packed up their ugly masks and manners and went right along with them.

Tales which frightened children thrived like none other. Engraved with a steely point upon young minds they were remembered and passed on down to new generations of young.

Thus but a few years ago in the lofty hills of North Carolina's Macon County there prowled a horned demon which seemingly obtained his name from his long sharp claws. When misty black clouds or damp dense fog swirled about the tall hills making them as black as hades *Old Scratch* with the long sharp claws rode the howling winds to the solitary cabins nestled beside eternally roaring streams of the falling valleys.

Standing upright upon his cloven hoofs he pried at the stout wooden doors barred safely with heavy wooden latches; and failing there he scratched and tugged at the tiny bolted windows while his flashing red eyes peered through at the sleeping children. Before retiring with the storm or the crow of the cock Old Scratch went about scratching, prying for a place of entry.

Next morning parents, observing marks left by the unwelcome visitor, might call to their children and point to the mud and stick chimney and say, "Look at them claw marks . . . better mind out . . . Old Scratch might get in tonight." (B12).

Hordes of Evil Spirits

Across the countless miles which stretch the length and breadth of North Carolina and its borders Old Scratch was not alone in terrorizing children. Surviving in the folk tradition are many malevolent spirits which have taken frightful appearances and adopted scary behavior.

One group goes under the many aliases of the Devil; some are descended from Old World demons; some are cloaked in the form of certain native birds and beasts; and some are a new breed of demons which are indigenous to the New World, being borrowed from the Indian or created by metamorphis from the ghosts of deceased evil human beings.

His Majesty, Prince of Fright

As with Old Scratch, the *Prince of Darkness* or *Prince of Fright,* commonly is represented to the young ones in a variety of forms.

In Martin County, upon the coastal plains, the Devil takes the appearance of the Scottish *Scarecrow.* In the Free Union community near Dardens where many of the people claim to be of free Negro and Tuscarora Indian descent, the Devil and some of his agents still appear to horrify the children. Andrew Pierce, keeper of a general store, says that to represent the Devil one dresses in ragged clothes, attaches sticks to his head for horns, and paints his face red like an Indian demon. When as frightful as the painted Indian warrior of a few centuries ago the *Devil* makes a quick appearance some distance from a group of children, makes a noise to draw their attention, and swells with diabolical joy as they scatter in terror. (P9).

On Knott's Island, Currituck County, settled by early English immigrants, His Majesty, the *Devil,* was "described to the children by the old people as an unsightly black monster." This county borders the Atlantic Ocean and the island, until 1804, could be reached by Currituck Inlet. Children were told that it had been visited by the Devil's agents, Blackbeard and Bluebeard. (A3, VII, 1, July 1959, pp. 4, 12).

In Martin County *Old Nick* was an old hairy man with a bull's head and horns, and he brought switches for parents to use on bad children. (B2).

Some of the Devil's names are more or less descriptive of his appearance. As *Old Red Eyes* his red displate eyes flame like the raging fires of hell. (B12). As *Old Black Boy* and *Old Black Sambo* he is the chief demon of the dark underworld. Upon the coastal plains in Bladen County the latter is a little black man with flashing red eyes. He might be seen walking down the road with a walking stick. (P8). As *Old Hob* he is related to the hobgoblins and has their frightful appearance. Usually he is a badly deformed hunchback with tiny horns on his head who walks with a limp. In Washington County, about 1880, *Bloody Bones* was a devil form represented as "a crippled little old man with a hunch back, cleft foot, and a horn on his head. (S2). But in Macon County *Bloody Bones* is the skeleton of a human body stripped of most of its flesh by the Devil. (B12).

Some of the Devil's other names are descriptive of his character. Most commonplace of these are the *Old Bad Boy* and the *Bad Man*. As these he is no great terror, and he may be called on to discipline children too young and tender for other forms.

Just a few decades ago some people were so fearful of the Devil that they did not care to mention his name outright, and they might use a mild alias instead. One might fear that the widely quoted proverb might be true: "Speak of the Devil and he will appear." Or should he be too tied up with other business his imps would appear. (B19, I, p. 193).

Year after year since those long ago years when the itinerant preacher plod dim pathways of beast infested forests to convert the shaggy frontiersman from inherent beastliness to spiritual cleanliness many of the Devil's aliases have been useful in representing the Devil's foul character. These stuck in children's minds like molasses taffy to their fingers. They include Satan, Lucifer, Belzebub, The Evil One, The Wicked One, The Arch Fiend, The Anti-Christ, The Adversary, The Old Serpent, The Old Dragon, Old Hairy, Old Nick, Belial, Mephisto, Mephistophles and so on.

Servants and Agents of the Devil

A class of scary supernaturals, seemingly descended from the hosts of medieval devils, are so widely dispersed that one is tempted to believe that wherever any European settler went those spirits were bound to go.

They are the goblins and hobgoblins which the observance of Halloween helps to keep alive; the bogies with several aliases, like bogie man, bogie bear, bogie boes; buggers and the Devil's imps, devoted servants and agents which look like the Devil in miniature and possess his evil character.

A group of less common, or local, evil spirits survive in the lore. In Washington County *Raw Head and Bloody Bones* is a horned little devil with a hunch back and cleft foot. (S2).

At Rodanthe in Dare County *Old Buck* is a beast-like demon with terrible long horns which shoots forth fire from his nostrils and roars like a northeaster. He comes at Old Christmas to annihilate Santa Claus. (W2, X, 1, p. 23).

In Hertford County the *Bogie Bear* is a small, black ugly spirit which molests bad children. (L15). In Halifax County he may take any form and make any noise he chooses. He is always ugly, if ever seen, and always in the form of a beast or a bird. He makes mysterious and uncanny noises at will, sometimes like the hoot or screech of an owl. (V3).

In Hertford and Bertie counties *Hell Hounds* are the Devil's bad dogs or demons in human form. (B10).

The Indigenous Demons

A group of demon-like beings which, like the bogies, take as great delight in frightening children are indigenous to the American frontier. They may have been inspired by Indian monsters, modeled after frightful animals and birds, or in some instances taken from both.

The antiquity of some of this lore may be seen in the imagery. The eerie cries of wolves by night, in Currituck County howling for human blood (A12), struck fear in hearts of frontier women and children. Virtually all wolves had been destroyed by 1750. But *The Wolf* as a beastly phantom still prowls remote parts of Pasquotank County. Sometimes there comes a knocking on the side of the house, and someone will see big eyes peeping through the window and tell frightened children, "Look . . . hear him! See him!" (B5).

The Bear may crush a man to death in his strong arms, and for a long time he has been stealing children and taking them into the deep swamps. (M13).

The panther, king of the forest had been destroyed by the early 1800's, but *The Panther* as a phantom spirit still lingers in some of the great woods of the coastal plains.

The *Hoop Snake*, mentioned by Lawson in 1609, still lurks in the lore almost everywhere, eager to roll like a hoop after his prey and strike it with his deadly sting.

The mythic *Coach Whip* lies in wait seeking an opportunity to whip man or beast to the bone. In slavery days some slaves were said to have preferred the master's harsh whip to a lashing by this snake. In Macon County people are whipped to death. When a whipped person faints the snake runs his tail up his nostrils to see if he is still breathing. (B12).

The Devil's Horse takes the form of the praying mantis. The demon can spit in a person's eyes from a great distance as straight as a bullet even in a hurricane and blind him. (B12).

Water Monsters inhabit the dark and deep waters of the coastal plains in the form of a water horse, alligator or giant snake. (B10; P9).

The Black Snake crawls down the throat of an infant after milk he has drunk.

When the slave mother left her infant in a basket at the end of a row *The Eagle* might come and steal him away.

The Turkey Buzzard just a few years ago sat in a dead tree beside the farm ready to pick out the eyes of those young girls who did not wear their bonnets. (L8).

The Shike Poke came to Hertford County from south New Jersey. This is a mythic bird-like creature which lives in the spung, pocosin, or swamp; has long legs and neck and utters an eerie cry. It carries naughty children away to its nest in the forest wastelands. (M11).

Humans Turn Demons

An assortment of violent and mysterious seeming people in both life and death have enriched folklore as frightful beings. They range from the solitary deformed recluse, hunched and hobbed like the Devil, the withered spinster, haggard like the broom-riding hag, to the demon-like spirit of the lifeless outlaw.

Almost every community has had its kindly *John Rhoady,* a small deformed black man who clattered

The Indian's 'Flying Head'.

through the village in a small rickety cart drawn by a small bony mule. (B5; V2).

Mote T, the hunch back Indian man of Plymouth fascinated children with wild tales, but people said he conversed with spirits. One could terrorize a child by threatening to tell him of their misdeeds. (P9).

The lifeless *Doughface*, like the Indian mask, became alive and turned a gentle person into a demon. (P12).

More than a century ago the village urchin of Williamston in Martin County "could tell a witch as far as we could see one." She appeared in the form of a wrinkled little old woman wearing bright scarlet cloak and hood, the better if she was shaking with palsy. She always was up to mischief. (R3, pp. 79-80).

The Wild Man was known to most communities. In some localities he was a beast-like creature which "made out like a man." Usually he had long tusks, long finger nails, long toe nails and was hairy all over. (P9). In some instances a bear stole him as an infant and raised him in the ways of the wild. (Y1; S4; S6).

The Old Hary Man of Free Union community, Martin County, is a beastly supernatural similar in appearance to the Tuscarora Indian's *Flying Head*. His long streaming hair serves him as wings. He flies about the forests and frequently comes to the borders of his dark sanctuary peering, looking and seeking to bring misfortune to people. (P9; J6, I, pp. 72-72).

The coastal Indians northward to New England had a mythic creature known as *The Hairy Man*. John Gyles, an Indian captive 1689-1698, quoted an old squaw as saying that when she was a girl she had known young persons to be taken away by this demon. (G10, pp. 2122; D5, pp. 286, 288).

Spirits of men who onetime led lives of violence may be especially diabolical. Among these are *Jesse James* and *Nat Turner*. Extravagant tales of robbing and killing by the James gang were widely circulated and Jesse's name became synonymous with violence. One girl was terrified when her grandfather threatened to tell the legendary outlaw about her misbehavior. (W3). For more than a century the ghost of Nat Turner, the widely publicized Southampton County, Virginia, insurrection leader, has been represented as diabolical. One hundred or more miles from the insurrection scene children might be threatened with "*Old Nat* (the child killer) will get you if you are bad." (J5, pp. 187-188).

Early in the twentieth century in Currituck County, North Carolina, the children greatly feared the spirits of *Blackbeard* and *Bluebeard*. They were represented as agents of the Devil and might appear at any moment. (A3, p. 12).

The Kingdom of Darkness—by Nathaniel Crouch, 1688.

PART IV
Acts of the Devil

10.

The Devil's Importance

THE most important figure in the New World folk tradition is the Devil.

Little wonder; he stands ready, is ever anxious, to satisfy the whims, fancies and cravings of everyone. He is one thing to one person and at the same time entirely something else to another. He justifies an unending struggle for improvement of man.

In North Carolina alone there are no less than twenty-eight places bearing his name. These include crooked and troublesome waterways, dark and secretive swamps, rugged mountain terrain, and land made sterile from his frequenting a particular place. (P15, pp. 141-142; J7).

In one North Carolina folklore collection thirty-eight proverbs proclaim his popularity. In some of these man seeks to imitate him and in others man alludes to his elusive appearance and character. For example, a man may be as mean as the devil; as crazy, cute, hot, mad, naughty, quick, ugly, wicked as the devil and at the same time drive like, feel, fight, look, run and work like the Devil. All the while he must give the Devil his due. (B19, I, pp. 392-394).

The Devil is able to manifest himself to the eyes of man in any form that is imaginable by man himself. And throughout the centuries man has made few exceptions as his mind has ranged from starched sobriety to lunacy.

Thus the form that he takes tells us as much about the man as it does the demon. In order to mislead, he may assume the form of a man or woman and animal; and he seeks to assume incredible and impossible shapes. In order to frighten those who would be wayward he assumes a form suited to instill terror.

The Devil appears in many colors, but most often in black, which suggests his place of abode. He most often is lean in stature. His eyes usually are saucer like, all black or sparkling red like coals. He generally is hairy, thus called Old Hairy, and sometimes has a hump on his back.

Once the Devil appeared to Martin Luther as a monk, but while conversing with him Luther observed that "the hands of the monk was like birds' claws." After being vanquished by a verse from the Scripture, the Devil "fled in a rage and growling." (R4, p. 51).

In England of a century ago the Devil could not take the form of a lamb, and of the birds he could simulate only the crow and the drake. (H5, pp. 240-41).

In the New World the Devil often appears in the form of beasts of the forest and at times he disguises himself in human form. A few years ago in the Indian Woods section of Bertie County, North Carolina, he came down the road as a sport, dressed in a pinstripe suit, a stove pipe hat and yellow shoes. (S6).

In the New England witch trials one Ann Foster said that the Devil appeared to her in the shape of a strange bird which had "two legs and great eyes." He "came white and vanished away black." (F3, pp. 247-248).

Cotton Mather observes that ordinarily the Devil appeared as a small black man. Witches had "their specters or devils, commissioned by them and representing them" to visit torments upon the people. (M3, pp. 80-84).

The Indian warriors of North Carolina, says Lawson, "paint their Faces all over red, and commonly make a Circle of Black about one Eye and another Circle of White about the other" while daubing their faces with clay, lamp-black, black lead and other colors to make themselves to seem "more like Devils than Human Creatures." (L2, p. 204).

Late in the eighteenth century the Reverend William Glendenning, a minister who traveled the North Carolina and Virginia border counties, claimed to have confronted the Devil several times. In one apparition:

"He appeared upward of five feet high,—round the top of his head there seemed a ridge,—some distance under the top of his head, there seemed a bulk, like a body, but bigger than any person;—about 15 or 18 inches from the ground, there appeared something like legs, and under them, feet; but no arms or thighs. The whole as black as any coal; only his mouth and eyes as red as blood. When he moved, it was as an armful of chains rattling together."

During some appearances he would shoot out of his head something like a horn, about six or eight inches high, above the top of his head." One time he appeared "like a four-footed beast, as large as a calf of a year old, and seemed to have large wings." (G2, pp. 19-25).

As the nineteenth century opened Theophilus Gates, who was to visit Virginia and North Carolina as an evangelist, saw the Devil as a colored man. As he passed in the night "I saw no motion of the body; but he passed swiftly, and seemed like any thing wafted along by the air." (G1, p. 8).

Evangelistic efforts of the eighteenth and nineteenth centuries gave the Devil immense importance. Thus it was only appropriate that he be represented as an ugly monster in sympathy with moral evil.

This popularity must have diverted much of the interest which had been held in the many demons, fairies, brownies and other spirits which had been brought over from Europe. Only a few of these retained their names in popular traditions. They also had to compete for favor with hordes of ghosts which began to flock from the cemeteries and dark and secluded places.

Washington Irving and other noted writers utilized this widespread interest in the Prince of Evil. In 1824 Lem Sawyer of Pasquotank County gave him an important role in his dramatic comedy *Blackbeard*. He appeared as the chief character in a variety of folk tales. To this day some story tellers are making practical use of his continuing popularity. Parents call upon him to make their children bid their wishes, and this usage alone has produced a vast amount of folklore. What child hasn't heard of the *bogy bear?*

11.
The Devil Comes for His Own

Appetite for Souls

In most parts of North Carolina and neighboring states the Devil has an insatiable appetite for souls. He may appear at the bedside of a dying person not looked over by a guardian angel. If the dying has led a wicked life, the Devil may make a dramatic appearance and carry his victim bodily down to the burning pit.

Paul Green, in his Cape Fear Valley folklore collection, tells of how he came as the *Old Black Boy* for the soul of a sinner. After tiptoeing into the death room "something like a big white moth" flew out of the dead man's mouth, and the *Old Black Boy* grabbed it with his two paws. He then sped off into the night "whickering and laughing." (G7, pp. 26-27).

Most of the deceased may sleep in death until the *Day of Judgment*. At this time, according to an old colored man, no sinner will escape the Devil: "When Christ comes to judge the world the sun will rise and get an hour high and it will be blown out. Then Gabriel will blow his trumpet and all the good people will rise. After they have gone to heaven the Devil will come with his *Hell Hounds* and chase the bad people into hell." (B10). From out of such a dark and awful threat came the folk song:

Wake up sinner, wake up quick;
I hope you ain't lying at Hell's dark door.

And to stay out of the clutches of the Devil one must ever keep in front of him. Should the old schemer appear in front of one in any form one must turn around and go back. (B10).

The Devil Comes for Old Jerry (BA)

Some of the Devil's appearances are made quite realistic by the story tellers as in this tale from Brunswick County, Virginia:

"You know," said informant Littleton Dromgoole, "the Devil comes in all kinds of forms . . . a man with all kinds of suits of clothes, except I ain't never hear tell of him wearing *overhauls* (overalls) . . . never hear of him in work clothes. He's a dude, and he likes flashy things. That's when he wants to tempt and lead folks his way.

"And a heap of times he comes like animals, like when he's in the woods or coming at night.

"When I was a boy near Lawrenceville in Brunswick County, Virginia, he made himself like a bear when he come after a wicked farmer, who lived a little ways down the road from us, and he come on dark nights, come several nights; that man fought him off.

" He was James Jerry, and people called him Old Jerry, for he must have been pushing eighty. The children were scared of them big earrings in his ears.

"Old Jerry's soul must have already belonged to the Old Bad Boy. He drank lots of whiskey, was as wicked as he could be, and he cussed all the time . . . would get up and cuss in the middle of the night.

"But Old Jerry must not have been all bad. Come Sunday he would hitch up his two-horse wagon and carry his wife to church.

Coming at Old Jerry was a black hairy thing.

"The Devil didn't start coming until Old Jerry got sicklified. Old Jerry must have had a notion that he would be coming, for he had his wife put the Bible beside the water pitcher on the table at his bedside.

"Then one night, a dark night, Old Jerry was lying flat of his back in bed when the house door flew open, and in rushed something like a big gust of wind. Old Jerry looked and coming at him was a big black hairy thing like a bear; and his eyes flashed flashes of fire.

"Old Jerry grabbed the *Good Book* off the table; he put it between him and the Devil; he shook it at him; and he say, 'Git back! Git back! Git back!' And the Devil's eyes they flash, and the Devil backs away. Then Old Jerry said, 'Git out! Git out! Git out of my house!' and the Devil go away.

"But soon Old Jerry hear his dogs fighting; they were in a terrible fight. He loved to fox hunt, and he had a whole passel of hounds. He loved them dogs; so he jumped up out of bed in his night clothes and ran out to look after his dogs. But he forgot to take the Bible with him. The Devil chased him right back into the house; then the Devil whipped all of them dogs down . . . killed two of them. All the fuss didn't stop until Old Jerry came out with his shotgun and shot over the Devil's head, then cried, 'That was buck lead, but next time it's going to be buck silver.' Then Old Jerry hears something heavy-footed like a horse galloping across the field toward the woods.

"My father say . . . he was Beauregard Dromgoole . . . he say the Devil must have gotten Old Jerry in the end. Every dark night after that he would come, but Old Jerry he stand him off with the Bible.

"Soon Old Jerry dies, and I suppose he can't stand the Devil off any more." (D6).

— *Littleton Dromgoole.*

The Devil Comes for Recluse (WA)

Years ago, folks have forgotten how long, a man lived in Indian Woods, Bertie County, North Carolina, who was so mysterious and wicked that people all over the county talked about him.

Except for a big black tom cat with flaming red eyes, he lived alone two miles off the main road on the edge of Roquist Pocosin. Hunters said that many a time they had shot at but could never seem to hit the cat.

This man wouldn't associate with people; and folks said he hated everything, he even hated children and animals. He only loved his black cat. Still folks invited him to church, corn shuckings and such like; but he wouldn't go.

Then he grew old and feeble; folks knew he didn't have much time left; and someone went by his cabin every now and then. And when he was taken with his mortal illness folks all around the neighborhood lived up to their custom of looking after the sick. They brought him food, the granny women doctored him, and folks went and sat and looked after his wants.

Then the granny women passed out the word. His time had come very near; their herb medicines no longer could help him. And more people than usual for a wake came to sit while his soul passed into eternity.

Death came one dark and drizzly night, it came far along about one or two o'clock when folks didn't stir from their homes except when necessary.

As the man struggled for breath one sitter looked out and said, "Wonder who that is coming . . . coming at this time?"

The light flared to blinding brilliance.

Others came and watched a glowing red light approach.

"Somebody has lost his way, he's coming through that brier thicket," one observed.

As the light drew near the man's breathing stopped. And the whole house looked. Suddenly the light grew quite large, far too large for a pitch pine torch, several pitch pine torches.

It moved as a red ball of fire, up and down and then to and fro. It came directly toward a window. It entered the room and flared to blinding brilliance and died out.

The sitters rubbed sight back into their eyes. All were shocked. The dead man and his bed were gone.

A conjure man mumbled what all knew to be true, "The Devil has come for his own." He seized a sedge broom, thrust it into the fireplace and put the cabin to the torch.

For a long time after that, people said, the woods all about the place smelled of sulphur. The black tom cat? No one saw or heard of him after that. (M7).

—*Judy Godwin (Mrs. Ernest) Mizelle.*

A Little Man Pretties the Pretty Girl (WA)

"When I was a girl living with my parents in the old Pettigrew house on Lake Phelps, Tyrrell County," says Dot Ainsley Cowan, "my grandmother, Mary Ellen Sawyer, told me many stories.

"One that made a lasting impression on me was one which she said her grandmother Phelps told her when she too was a girl. It must have been well over a hundred years ago.

"A very pretty girl about my age at the time be-

The visitor busied himself with hair curlers.

came ill, and all efforts of the herb women could not save her.

"It was a sad occasion, according to Granny Phelps. Although her family was poor her beauty had made her vain. Each Sunday morning while other folks were at church she would sit and curl her hair until each flowing lock was in place. She wouldn't listen to her mother when she warned that curling her hair on Sunday was a sin. She could do it on Saturday instead.

"The family, who loved and admired her, wanted a fine casket with a glass top on it, but they were too poor. So local carpenters built her a box of cypress lumber with a nail-on-lid. But these craftsmen hand-planed the exterior to a smooth freshness.

"Neighbors came to sit with her remains until time for burial and nailing on of the coffin lid.

"At night many of her young friends came for the wake. The coffin remained open that all who wished might view her remains. Those who did so remarked that she was as beautiful in death as she had been in life and that she seemed to be in a peaceful sleep.

"Deep in the night one of the sitters looked up from a noisy game and saw beneath the pale candlelight something like a little man sitting beside the casket. Then others looked, and all choked up with silence. For the visitor with pointed ears and horned head was busy with hair curlers.

"The sitters were so frightened that they streamed from the room. When they returned the little man was gone. And they found the dead girl's hair waving alive with flowing curls.

"All present shuddered when one viewer said, 'He must have been the Devil prettying her up for her journey with him.' "   (C9).

—*Dot Ainsley (Mrs. Jack) Cowan.*

A Warning for the Two Uncles (WA)

"I adored my grandmother, Lula Hardee, who lived near us in Scotland County, near Laurinburg, when I was a girl." A great-grandmother had lived in Columbus County and she had family connections in several neighboring counties.

"I admired by grandmother for her wisdom and the many folksy stories she would tell me. Each and every one had a moral point. For example, the *whipping snake*, which sometimes was called the *coachwhip*, did not chastise good children. Then there was the *stinging snake*, sometimes called the *hoop snake*, which was to be feared much as a demon.

"But the story which impressed me most was the moral lesson that my uncles Hubbard and Henry Hardee learned when they were no more than sixteen years old.

"There was a married man in the community, I never learned his name, who was running out on his wife. He got to taking my uncles along as a front. He'd go to the bootlegger, get some whiskey and leave them outside drinking while he went in to see his girl friend.

"Uncle Henry and Uncle Hubbard were getting in a mighty bad way, said Grandma, when their warning came. When the man brought them home one night there was a large red light in the top of a tree at the edge of the yard. Then that light turned loose and fell to the ground right in front of them. They stood still, frozen in their tracks, scared nearly to death. Before you could blink your eyes the light went out and in its place was an animal-like thing about the size of a big cat . . . hairy . . . had big red eyes . . . that seemed to sparkle all over with red flashes of fire.

"Grandma heard the commotion and came to the door. When she opened it the thing ran by her and up the stairway. The whole family was looking and all saw it. By now everybody was scared; but they crept upstairs after the thing. They moved Uncle Hubbard's and Uncle Henry's bed. It had gone under the bed, but they found nothing.

"Grandma warned her two boys; that was the Devil after them.

"And I felt that her warning stuck. After hearing the story I looked upon Uncle Hubbard and Uncle Henry with awe. I had known them as good law abiding men.

"And I was glad that the Devil didn't get them." (B18).

—*Carol Smith (Mrs. Howard) Brown.*

Grandma Saves Sammy (BA-J)

"Before my grandmother died," says a fifteen-year-old, "she told me about a boy named Sammie. He was mean. He gambled, drank whiskey, cursed and did stuff like that. And she told him he ought not to be so mean; something might happen to him.

"One day Sammie was cursing and carrying on, and all of a sudden he went to sleep. His mother heard something walking inside the house. She looked and she saw Sammie going out the door with the Devil.

"Sammie's mother ran out there in the yard, and she looked and saw the Devil carrying Sammie under the house. She grabbed the yard broom and beat

If Grandma hadn't beat the Devil off!

the Devil off. Then she took Sammie back into the house.

"When Sammie got back like himself again she told him he had better stop being so mean. But he still talks with the Devil. They talks about cards, gambling, drinking, girls, fighting and stuff like that." (S8).

—*Wesley Snead.*

The Little Red Spots (BA-J)

According to a fourteen-year-old, "This man did bad things, like drinking and using profane language, during the day; and his wife told him he had better stop. But he kept right on.

"That night he went to sleep and the Devil came to get him. The Devil come with long horns and a forked tail, and he had a pitch fork.

"The Devil chased the man out of bed, and they ran around and around the room. And every time the Devil got close he would punch the man with his pitch fork, and the man would cry, 'Ouch! ouch!'

"The Devil got so hot on the man that he ran out the door, and the Devil chased him around the house three times before the man ran back into the house and slammed the door.

"Then the man went to the window and looked out. There was the Devil looking all around. And when the Devil saw the man looking at him he *blinked away*.

"That man still has got little red spots all over him where the Devil stuck him with his pitch fork." (W13).

—*Shelton Williams.*

The White Chariot (WA)

"I knew Old Sam Ellis of Lunenburg County, Virginia. He died of old age after a long and colorful life," says William I. Marable.

Sam had served the Ellis family in slavery, and then he complained that freedom brought him more troubles than it took waay. As he grew old he found comfort in reading the Scriptures. He put aside a part of his deviltry, like chicken stealing, and became very religious.

"And the Devil didn't like it," Sam would say. "He thought he had me for good, and now I'm doing all I can to stay out of his clutches."

The Archenemy, according to Sam, kept picking on him in hopes that he would backslide. So he began to pray to the Lord to lend a hand through his Providence and relieve him of his earthly troubles.

In Sam's later years life became so burdensome that he would conclude his prayers with the plea "... and Good Lord send your white chairiot down to take poor old Sam out of this sinful world."

Now, Sam delighted in regaling his listeners, especially young folks, with tales about the mysterious workings of the supernatural; and he unnerved himself by the excesses of his own tales. It wasn't often that one found him away from his cabin after nightfall. Here he might be found warming his old bones before the fire or sitting reading his dog eared Bible.

But one time night overtook Sam several miles from home on lonely Old Fort Mitchell Road near the old fort site. By his own admission he was a bit afraid. The road was bordered by deep woods most of the way home; the night was dark and damp, the kind through which eerie echo-like sounds might bounce and crowd in from all directions.

Eventually there came a clearer and more inviting sound. It followed the dirt roadway at a distance, and it seemed like the drumming of many horses' hoofs together with a rumbling like that of carriage wheels. "Maybe somebody will give Old Sam a ride," Sam quoted himself as wishing. Soon this sound also grew disturbing; it was approaching too swiftly; and the beating grew louder and louder until it was like the booming wings of a bevy of partridges.

"Dis ain't natural!" Old Sam promptly reminded himself. And he didn't have long to wait to see. It came bearing down on him.

"Here it come . . . here come a white chariot . . . four white horses snorting and pawing the air . . . and up dere driving wuz a big white creature . . . no hands, no legs . . . jest a-floating and a-waving."

Sam fled. "Boss, I git away from there . . . when I feels that hoss' breath I jest leaves 'em."

That broke Sam from asking for a free chariot trip to the *Pearly Gates*. He explained, "Boss, de Debbil mus' hear me, and when he cotch me out dat night he pull dat trick on me." (M1).

—*William I. Marable.*

The Devil at the Spring

Shortly after the Civil War one Will Carpenter roamed the country about Crouse in Lincoln County, North Carolina. For reasons plain to the naked eye he was known as Big Foot Billy. The tracks of his great bare feet left imprints on the dusty roads, zig-zag fashion, for Big Foot Billy didn't have it in him to walk a straight line. If he wasn't roaring drunk he was having the shakes, and a man with the shakes as Billy had them is a wavering subject.

He considered seasoned whiskey hogwash; weak, puny stuff not fit to dose the children with. It was all right with Billy if the inns refused him entrance to the taproom. What he liked was a woodland clearing cozily furnished with vat and coil, where he could catch in a dipper the diamond drops that seared his innards so pleasantly. It took a weary while to get a dipperful, but the stuff was worth the trouble.

One summer night he wandered to the Huffstetter boys' still two or three miles southeast of Lincolnton and a few miles further from his home.

After a time he felt aglow and like himself again. He wanted to lie down. Though his cornshuck bed was miles away he plodded homeward singing songs sweet to his ears.

The full moon shone bright, and as he neared the spring near McLeod's farm he saw a brilliant light, too lustrious to be the moon, reflected in the spring water. As he drew closer it seemed to be a great fire, then he saw that it was a fire with the Devil sitting in the middle of the flames.

The Devil squatted there blinking his lashless eyes at Big Foot. In one hand he had a pitchfork and in the other a loop of red-hot chains. He was mother-naked, of a soft reddish brown color, with two little sawed-off horns sprouting from his forehead. The end of his tail was split like the tongue of a snake. Big Foot snapped to and started to run. Alas, his big feet were anchored to the earth. He couldn't budge. The heat was awful.

"I've come after you, Billy," the Devil said. "With all that alcohol soaked in you you'll burn beautifully."

Billy fell to his knees.

"Please, suh, don't do that, Devil," he begged again and again.

The Devil grinned and moved his flaming body closer. Billy thought he was doomed to be roasted alive.

"I'll be good! I'll never touch another drop of liquor," he shouted. "I'll be the best man in Lincoln County."

The Devil thought a minute and then laughed out loud. "All right," he said, "we'll make a bargain. I know that without a drink you'll be in a worse hell than mine. Go free this time. But watch out! If I ever see you drunk again I'll come back after you."

Billy turned tail and ran. Upon reaching home he waked up his family to tell them the story. His brothers, not believing any of it, made him go back to the spring. There was no trace of the Devil. But some of them did claim that the ground was rather warm on the spot where Billy swore the Devil had been.

From that night on Big Foot Billy turned teetotaler. Many years later, after a long period of fine health, he died a man of sanctity.

Even today they call that place the Devil's Spring. (B4).

—*Memry Baker.*

The Devil's Sting (BA)

Six months before the end of time . . . end of the world . . . the Great Evil Spirit . . . the Devil . . . he come out like a locust . . . with wings . . . sting in tail . . . go around to these churches.

If you are a sinner, he'll sting you in the forehead. You beg to die and can't die. Death come to and flee from you . . .

The Devil may try the Christian, but he can't sting him. He like a bee around blossoms . . . won't bother those flowers he can't feed on.

He fly right to them but fly right on by them . . . one, two, three, four or five until he come to a sinner. . . . (B10).

—*Edward Beverly.*

The Devil's Invitation (BA)

When a person dies and there comes a storm behind you . . . that lumbering, that thunder rolling you hear is the sound of the Devil meeting of you.

The Devil is inviting you . . . your spirit . . . into his house . . . into hell. Hell is his house. (B10).

—*Edward Beverly.*

12.

The Devil and the Preacher

Where You Find the Devil

The Devil in folklore, as the *Old Adversary*, devotes untiring efforts to discrediting the preacher and nullifying his work, as in this tale from Hoke County, North Carolina:

One Saturday a preacher was talking to a man, asking him to come to church on Sunday. While talking a third man — the Devil who appeared as a man— came up and said, "The preacher is telling you right; you do like he tell you, you go to church on Sunday; but today you go with me."

The fellow went with the Devil, and when night come and the sun went down the Devil had him.

It wasn't very long after that before the preacher told the Devil, "Why, hello there; I thought you were gone from this town.'"

The Devil told him, No."

Then the preacher asked, "Where were you last Sunday?"

"I was at the church; I was up in the *Amen Corner* where the deacons were—between the deacons and the preacher—to see what I could get on to up there." And he say, "If you come to church you'll find me, but you'll never find me back in that back crowd at the door. I wuz up there with the preacher to see what's going on, to see what I can get into."

Preacher say the reason he wasn't at church that Sunday was because he was out looking for the Devil. He went to all the bootlegger places, and went out in dancing places and then went to all the whore houses and couldn't find him nowhere and dey didn't know he had gone out of this country.

And the Devil say, "If you had come to church you would have found me there. I was sitting in the Amen Corner up there amongst the deacons seeing what I could get into up there—seeing what was going on." Say, "You find me up there in the deacons' seat between them and the preacher." The Devil never back there in the back seat with the sinners. (S4).

—*Jim Shaw.*

The Devil Whips the Preacher (WA)

An old colored preacher was going to church one Sunday with his Bible, and the Devil came out of the woods and said to him, "I can whip you." And the man said, "No you can't either, because I have got the Lord on my side."

So the Devil tackled the preacher. But the preacher held to his Bible with his left hand and whipped the Devil with his right hand.

So the Devil got up and went back into the woods and hollered back, "You'll lose your strength and I'll whip you before you get to church."

The preacher said, "No you won't, for I still got the Lord's strength with me."

A little further on the Devil came from the woods again and the preacher licked him again, in the same way.

So the Devil slunk off into the woods again and hollered back, "I'm still going to get you, for you are losing faith."

The third time the Devil came out of the woods as the man was trudging along, and this time he said, "I know the reason why I can't whip you; you got that Bible in your hand."

By now the preacher had lost faith and decided to go on his own. He said, "No, you can't whip me," and he laid his Bible down.

Whereupon the Devil whipped him good.

Moral: Man is of little strength without the help of God. (F.4).

—C. B. Foutz

A Fight With the Devil (BA)

My father, Henry Johnson, was a colored evangelist preacher. He preached all the way from North Carolina to Florida. He used to tell us children about the time he was returning one night from holding a meeting an evil thing followed him through rocky country.

My father looked and saw that the thing stood on its hind feet like a kangaroo, and it struck at him with its front feet.

This was rough country, but there wasn't supposed to be anything like that here. So he decided that it must be the Devil. He told us that the old Devil can't stand up to iron, and that was the reason he always carried an iron tipped walking stick with him wherever he went.

So my father beat off that thing with his stick and then chased it behind some rocks where it disappeared.

He hurried on toward home, but the thing overtook him, and they had another fight.

As my father got near home he cried out to his family, "You all come meet me; I been fighting something two or three hours."

Next day in bright sunlight he went back over that path, and he found "scuffling tracks and cloven foot prints."

He was certain, my father said, that his Bible, his walking stick and his calm temper had saved him from being carried off by the Devil. (J1).

—Alex Johnson.

13.
Funning the Devil

The Farmer's Curst Wife (WA)
(*As sung with the dulcimer by Virgil Sturgis, Asheville, North Carolina.*)

There was an old farmer went out for to plow
   Hey ding daddle, ding daddle, ding day!
He hitched up his horse and his mule to the plow.
   Hey ding daddle, ding daddle, ding day!

The Devil came by with a flickety flack
And carried a pitch-fork wrapped up in a sack.
   Hey ding daddle, ding daddle, ding day!

The old farmer dropped his lines and he ran.
Said, "The Devil's looking for my only son!"
   Hey daddle, ding daddle, ding daddle, ding day!

"No, it ain't your son nor your daughter fair,
It's your old scolding wife, she I shorely must have."
   Sing daddle, ding daddle, ding daddle, ding day!

So he shouldered her up on his tired old back
And he looked like a pedler a-totin' his pack.
   Sing daddle, ding daddle, ding daddle, ding day!

He carried her down to the gates of hell,
Said, "Blow up the fire, boys, we'll roast her quite well."
   Sing daddle, sing daddle, ding daddle, ding day!

One little smoked devil looked over the wall,
Said, "Tak'er back, Daddy, she'll murder us all!"
   Sing daddle, sing daddle, ding daddle, ding day!

Seven little smoked devils came rattlin' their chains,
She up with her slipper and knocked out their brains.
    Daddle, sing daddle, sing daddle, ding day!

So he shouldered her up on his tired old back
And then down the road he went clickety-clack.
    Daddle, sing daddle, sing daddle, ding day!

He carried her down to the forks of the road,
Said, "Get down, Old Woman, you're a terrible load!"
    Daddle, sing daddle, sing daddle, ding day!

She was seven years goin', but six coming back
When she looked for the corn-pone she left in a crack.
    Daddle, sing daddle, sing daddle, ding day!

They found the old farmer asleep in his bed,
She up with a butter-stick and paddled his head.
    Sing daddle, ding daddle, ding daddle, ding day!

"Take her back, take her back, with all my heart,
I hope to my soul that you never will part."
    Sing daddle, sing daddle, ding daddle, ding day!

"Now I've been a devil most of my life,
But I never knew hell until I met your wife."
    Sing daddle, ding daddle, ding daddle, ding day!

"Now what I am good for, the Devil won't tell.
I ain't fit for heaven; I'm too mean for Hell."
    Daddle, sing daddle, sing daddle, ding day!

This all goes to show women are smarter than men.
They can go down to Hell and come back again!
    Hey ding daddle, ding daddle, ding day!

    —Courtesy of Virgil Sturgis, Asheville, N. C.,
    Originally the ballad was heard sung by
    a mountain woman near Swannanoa, N. C.

The Devil Picks on Uncle Ned

While traveling through North Carolina, Tennessee and other southern states in the 1850's David Hunter Strother, who wrote for *Harper's Monthly* under the pen name of *Porte Crayon*, provides a kind of devil humor that seems to have been enjoyed immensely during the period. He stopped for a visit with a gentleman whom he called Squire Broadacre. During his stay the Squire told him of a boyhood story about the troubles that one old Negro servant had with the Devil.

This old Uncle Ned was "old enough to be on the invalid list, and spent his days between his pigpen, his patch, and his prayers."

His wife, Aunt Betty, was "a capital cook," and the Squire, then a boy Tony, enjoyed "many a savory meal in her cabin." But his feasts were troubled with Uncle Ned's sermons and admonitions.

Although Uncle Ned was troubled little with ardous labor he had other troubles: "The archenemy of souls, it seems, had an especial spite on him, and had personally appeared to him in a variety of forms. . . . He had followed him in the shape of a black cat; had crawled into his cabin like a copper-snake, and tried to bite him; as a huge owl he had perched upon the roof, and scared him with his hootings. When he could do no beter, he manifested his disapprobation of the old martyr by spitting at him from among the coals in the fire-place."

As dark fell Tony took down his father's powder horn and went to Uncle Ned's cabin, crawled onto the roof, and leaned over the big stick chimney. "The hearth was glowing with a fine bed of coals, upon which sat a coffee-pot and a skillet frizzling with fat sausages. The old woman was fidgeting about the supper-table, while the old man was sitting in front of the fire enjoying the prospect, and possibly, reflecting on his sins.

"As I carefully dropped a few grains of powder upon the coals, he suddenly drew back his chair.

"'Betty, look da! See debbil sparklin' in dat fire da?'

"''Tain't nothin'; jis' a sign of snow.' And Betty went on with her preparations.

"'Betty,' cried old Ned, drawing still farther from the fire, ''pears to me I smells brimstone!'

"''Tain't nothin'' replied Betty, with less assurance than at first.

"A more decided blaze and smell of brimstone drove the old couple into the remotest corner of the room, where Ned, too much terrified to articulate a prayer, began to groan lustily. In my efforts to repress a sneeze, the next moment I let fall the horn. Whether I rolled or was blown off the roof of the cabin I can not tell, but in my bewilderment I gathered up and ran to the great house as fast as my legs could carry me. I slipped into the sitting-room where the family were gathered and took a back seat, that my agitation and rapid breathing might not be noticed.

"The next moment there was a sound of hurrying footsteps through the yard, on the porch, in the hall; the door burst open, and in rushed Uncle Ned, staring speechless. The inmates of the room started to their feet, when the old man's knees gave way, and he sunk at his old mistress's feet, grasping her gown with both hands. Aunt Betty followed, blown and frightened, but not speechless.

"'Oh marster! o marster! — Debbil arter us, sure enough!'

"The old negroes shook as if in an ague fit; but soothing words, with the assistance of a glass of cordial, partially restored their incoherent wits, and Aunt Betty was presently enabled to communicate the cause of their alarm.

"While she was cooking supper her old man had observed some signs in the fire he did not like; there was an onaccountable spitting and sputtering, and a strong smell of brimstone, which, he too well knew, indicated the presence of the Evil One. Ned tried to pray, but his tongue clove to the roof of his mouth; when all at once, with a clap of thunder and a cloud of fire, the foul fiend came down the chimney. With one hand he shied the coffee-pot at her head, and with the other hurled the skillet of sausage at her husband; then began with his shovel to toss chunks and coals over the room; and wound up by seating himself, cross-legged, on the old chest, and spitting streams of fire at them. 'On dat very chest whar de whiskey was,' sobbed Aunt Betty. 'I often told Ned dat whisky oughtn't be dar. Debbil knowed dat whiskey no business dar.'

" 'They're drunk!' cried my father. 'Get out, you old sinners! How dare you alarm the house with such nonsense?'

" 'Their terror is real,' replied my mother. 'George, Sam,' said she, addressing two negro men, 'go down to the cabin directly, and see what is the matter.'

" 'Mistis,' answered George, 'I'se afeard.'

"My father took his hat and stick, and, followed by a trembling posse of whites and blacks, went himself to examine the premises. Things were found in the cabin pretty much as Aunt Betty had described them, except that the notorious individual who had made all the mischief was gone. The cooking utensils and

What Aunt Betty Saw

supper were scattered over the house, mingled with coals and chunks of fire, and a cloud of sulphurous smoke not yet dispersed. My father looked bewildered, and the teeth of the negroes began to chatter at these unmistakable evidences of the recent presence of his Satanic Majesty.

"Presently Sam stooped to examine an object lying on the floor. 'Merciful Fathers!' he exclaimed, suddenly jumping back, 'it's one of he's horns!'

" 'What is it?' asked my father. 'Hand it to me.'

"Sam shuddered. 'Master, tell me to kill myself, and I'll do it; but I wouldn't touch dat—not for my freedom.'

"My father picked it up himself, and on examination it proved to be a veritable horn, much splintered and powder-burned.

" 'I smell a rat!' said my father, putting the horn in his pocket, and quietly leading the way back to the house.

"As I expected, I was presently called aside.

" 'Tony, this is the remnant of my big powder-horn. Explain this matter immediately.'

"I could not tell a lie to my father, even if I had been so disposed; so I told him the story from beginning to end without apology or circumlocution. He tried to look stern, but was evidently at some trouble to repress a laugh."

Tony was made to explain the whole matter to all, whites and blacks; some laughed, some mustered enough courage to take the horn in their hands, but Uncle Ned "never could be induced to cross the threshhold of his cabin again." (E1, pp. 274-276).

The Biggest Liar (BA-J)

Once upon a time the Devil caught three men — a yellow man, a white man, and a black man — and took them down to hell.

When they got there the men were very frightened and begged the Devil to let them go. So he say, "I will let the one go who can tell the biggest lie."

So he say to the yellow man, he was a Chinaman; he say to the Chinaman, "You git the first go."

The Chinaman started talking. He was so scared that he just jabbered. Even the Devil can't make out what he say. So he say, "Stand aside, that ain't no lying."

Next, the Devil say to the white man, "What is your lie?"

The white man started talking, and the Devil say, "That ain't no lie; stand aside."

So the Devil come to the black man, and he say, "Alright black boy, what is your lie?"

The black man was mighty scared seeing how the other two didn't make it. But he say, "Once I had a wreck." And he say, "My wife was lying east, my daughter was lying west, my son was lying south." Then he stopped.

Then the Devil say, "Where were you lying?"

And the black man say, "Boss, you knows I was lying all the time."

So the Devil had to let the black man go. (B3).

—*Rocky Bailey.*

14.

Outwitting the Devil

DURING the first half of the nineteenth century the Devil became an important figure in both literature and folklore. As time went on it became the fashion among some to subject him and those under his yoke to humor.

In such tales the master of cunning was outwitted by weaker mortals.

A common motif has the soul-hungry Devil wanting no one smarter than he to worry with in hell.

Such is the case of one Jack, an evil man, who outwits the Devil in all their dealings.

The people of the Beaufort, North Carolina, Woodstock community have a rhyme that tells of the Devil's pain when was outsmarted by one Dick. Mrs. Minnie Hollowell Allen heard it chanted by her grandfather, J. William Hall, 1857-1842:

> Dick and the Devil,
> They played for a smooth half dollar;
> Dick beat the Devil,
> And he took the money up;
> And the people over Jordan (spirits of the dead)
> Heard him holler. (A1).

How Kill Devil Hill Got Its Name

The Devil may be the only one who knows how Kill Devil Hill on North Carolina's Outer Banks got its name.

One legend explains that it came from a New England rum consumed in Carolina. In 1728 William Byrd of Virginia observed the rum was "so bad and unwholesome that it is not improperly called *Kill-Devil*." (B15, p. 92; P15, p. 264).

Another legend related by an unknown story teller gives an entirely different explanation:

—o—

Whence Kill Devil Hill derived its name has been the subject of some controversy, but one explanation of its origin has to do with a native fisheman of the Currituck Sound shore who sold his soul to the Devil for unlimited wealth.

Worn and weary with his hitherto fruitless struggle against grinding poverty, the fisherman lent a willing ear to tales of men who, by secret bargaining with the Prince of Darkness had become rich beyond the dreams of avarice. He consulted an old banker woman who was reputed to have held daily converse with the Devil, and from her learned the secret of the unholy rites by which the Evil One might be summoned.

To the summit of a neighboring hill at midnight came the Devil at the behest of the fisherman. The bargain was soon concluded; in exchange for the fisherman's soul, which at his death became the property of the Prince of Evil, the fisheman was to enjoy during his lifetime the possession of all the wealth that his heart desired. Full agreement reached, the Devil vanished as quickly as he came. His victim, exultant and happy in the possession of a bag of gold, the forerunner of others which Satan would bring to a meeting arranged for the fifth night following, returned to his hut at the foot of the hill and went to bed—but not to sleep. Visions of eternal torments drove slumber from him; all night he tossed and moaned, but with the dawn came courage and a plan whereby he might retain his wealth and yet cheat the Devil of his prize. He would lay a trap into which Satan would surely fall, and retain years of happiness and luxurious living which, as he thought, only wealth could secure.

To think was to act, and with four days and nights leeway before the next meeting, the fisherman went on the hilltop, carrying a spade. His plan was to dig there a grave so deep that it would reach the quicksand below the upper layers of earth. On the fourth night his task was completed and the fisherman awaited the appointed hour with confidence that the Devil would fall headlong into the grave, which he had carefully covered with the branches of trees, twigs, and leaves.

Came midnight of the fifth night, and with it the Devil, who found the fisherman awaiting him on the opposite side of the hidden grave. "Throw me the bag of gold," cried the fisherman, "and let us shake hands on the bargain." Over went the gold, and down went the Devil as he stepped on the flimsy covering of the grave; deep into the quicksand which swallowed him and all his works.

"I have killed the Devil," joyfully shouted the fisherman as he rushed down the hill to spread the news far and wide. (N16).

A Hell of Your Own (WA)

One time there was a blacksmith at Bath who was so worldly in his ways that the Devil often would come by to pay him a visit.

They were quite chummy until the man's health began to fade and the Devil said he'd be taking him down to hell after awile.

At that the blacksmith set to thinking how he could part company with his evil friend of long standing. And when the Devil came again the blacksmith proposed that they amuse themselves with some games.

The Devil put on his magic act, appearing in the form of different animals and things and was having a big time while the blacksmith seemed frightened half to death when he said, "I bet you can't change yourself into a dime, being I is thirsty for a shot of brandy . . . and you can change yourself back at the expense of the tavern keeper."

"No sooner said than done," said the Devil.

The blacksmith picked up the dime and put it on his anvil and began hammering him with a stamping iron in the shape of a cross.

"Ouch!" cried the Devil. "Stop that . . . take that iron off of me."

"I will if you promise to leave me alone and never take me to hell," and the blacksmith gave him a hard lick.

"Ouch!" cried the Devil again. "Stop it! stop it! I'll do anything you say. Just let me up from here."

The blacksmith took up his tool and the Devil flicked away. And he never did come back to the blacksmith's shop again.

After some time the blacksmith died. He was too wicked for heaven, so he went down to hell. When he got there the Devil wouldn't let him in. You're too smart for me," he chided him.

"Well, where can I go?"

"That's no matter for me."

"But this is where I am supposed to go!"

"Well, I'll tell you what I'm going to do. You are so smart I'm going to wind you up and send you over to the *Fiddler's Green* where you can have a hell of your own." (C1).

—*David Cahoon.*

Jack Outwits Father-in-Law (WA)

In Cherokee County a man by the name of Jack married the Devil's daughter, and immediately he found himself in a violent struggle with his father-in-law.

The Devil came in a rage. Jack pretended to cut his wife's throat, but he only cut a bladder filled with blood. The Devil flew home, tried the same thing on his wife and really cut her throat.

The Devil then squeezed up stones in his hands, but Jack squeezed up larger dumplings.

Eventually the Devil seized Jack, put him in a sack and set off for the river to drown him. The Devil left him by the road when he stopped at a house. Along came a man with a drove of hogs. Jack said he was on his way to heaven, and the man readily exchanged places with him.

The man was drowned, and the Devil was surprised to meet Jack, who said he had been to hell and back and got a drove of hogs. (B13, pp. 308-309).

The Sharp Landlord (WA)

In Sampson and Northampton counties, North Carolina, a tenant farmer had a dream in which he was given a guided tour of hell by the Devil.

In the Sampson account, one Jack Barefoot had lost both his crops and his land when Old Walt Casey, the landlord, got out his sharp pencil to figure up the "carrying charges."

Jack told his listeners that the Devil turned out to be quite obliging. He answered all his questions and treated him so nice he decided he wouldn't bother him by asking about a large washpot he had seen "turned up-side down, just inside the gate." As Jack reached down to grab a hook to take a peep, his host flew into a rage. "Satan then explained, " 'I got Walt Casey under there. You yourself know what 'ud happen, if he got loose. He'd have a mortgage on hell before nightfall!' " (M5, p. 18).

In the Northampton story, the Devil screamed, "Don't you do that! We've got old man Bridgers under there. If he gets out, it won't be long before he'll have a mortgage on hell." (V3).

The Little Girl and the Devil (BA)

Once a little girl tripped and spilled her pail of milk. Immediately along came the Devil and offered to help her for the price of her soul.

She agreed.

The milk instantly was returned to the pail, and the Devil asked for his pay.

The little girl danced on home to get it while the Devil changed himelf into the form of a shoat to await her return.

Soon she was back with the sole of an old shoe which she pulled from her pocket and threw at her old tempter. Startled and frightened the Devil took to his heels. (P5, p 203).

Sole Saves Her Soul (BA)

In an Elizabeth City County, Virginia, Negro tale, a little girl wanted so much to become an accomplished singer and dancer that she willingly pledged her soul to a little old man in behalf of his master, the Devil.

After twenty-eight years the Devil appeared and asked for her soul. She wished to save her real soul, so she threw an old shoe sole at the "ugly, man-like thing that did not know the difference." (P1, p. 282).

The Origin of 'Uh-huh' (BA)

A Hertford County, North Carolina, tale tells of the origin of *uh-huh*.

Once while visiting the earth the Devil gathered up all the souls of sinners that he could carry. He had his pockets and hands full, and he held some in his mouth. Still he wanted more. Someone asked him if he did not.

That caught him in a bind. He couldn't open his mouth to say "Yes," for the souls would drop out of his mouth and get away. So he grunted, "Uh-huh" instead.

Folks copied him, and they began to say "uh-huh" like the Devil did. (B10).

—Edward Beverly.

15.
Sundry Devil Tales

The Phantom Banjo Picker (BA)

When Jim Allen Vaughan of the Menola community of Hertford County, North Carolina, was a boy in the 1880's he wanted himself a banjo but he did not have enough money to buy one. So he decided to make one. He obtained a large gourd, cut out one side and covered it over with a shorn sheep hide. A white woman gave him a spool of cotton for the strings.

"I got so I could pick that thing right good, and I thought a whole heap of it," said Jim Allen, "but as you know the banjo is the Devil's music instrument. My music box got all crossed up."

About midnight one night Jim Allen was awakened by the noise of something picking his banjo. ."I could hear it real clear, but I could see no one. I knew the Devil liked to play the banjo; so I got real scared. I wrapped my head under the kiver. Next day I burned that thing up."

The Devil did not return after that. (V5).

—*Jim Allen Vaughan.*

The Guitar at the Funeral (BA-J)

"My Uncle, who lives out in the county from Murfreesboro, told me this," explained a thirteen-year-old.

"This dude was dead. He had been a good guitar

player, and he wanted the guitar played at his funeral. So they got this guitar player to play. He was in the church playing. When he finished his piece he laid the guitar down, and the guitar kept right on playing.

"My uncle said it did that because the guitar is an instrument of the Devil, and it is not supposed to be played in church." (V6).

—John Vaughan

The Devil in the Guitar (BA)

"Horace Futrell told me this, and I believe it," said Dallas Moore just a little while ago. "Horace has learned a lot and he tells it like it is."

Horace bought himself a guitar although his mother told him he couldn't have one. She wasn't having the Devil's music box in her house.

Horace hid his guitar beneath his bed thinking he could slip out with it at night and go playing with some other dudes who had guitars.

But when the family was at home sitting down to the table the guitar began to play. Everybody looks and can see nothing, but Horace's mother Julia goes and finds it.

" 'That thing has got the Devil in it,' she said, 'and I ain't going to let the Devil be hanging around this house.' " She told Horace to take his new guitar out to the woodpile and chop it up.

But Horace hid his guitar beneath some shucks in the corn crib. It had cost him too much for what he made toting out groceries at the grocery store.

But when Julia goes to the barn she hears that

guitar again. She makes Horace dig it out of the shucks and burn it.

"That happened several years ago. Horace is older now, and he says he wouldn't have a guitar in his house for nothing." (M10).

—*Dallas Moore.*

Accosts the Church Goer (BA)

One Sunday afternoon this man was coming from church walking and talking. Along his way he saw a low black thing in the road. As he came upon it he realized that it was the Devil.

"Where you from?" the Devil asked gruffly.

"I come from praying ground," replied the man.

"I don't believe it!" retorted the Devil.

The man had told the truth; and the Devil went on and left him alone.

Yet knowing what it was the man was so unnerved that he went on home shaking like a leaf. (B10).

—*Edward Beverly.*

The Little Boy on the Fence (BA-J)

"My uncle-in-law, who lives in Blackjack near Ahoskie, North Carolina, told me this," said the thirteen-year-old.

A long time ago this guy was driving a mule, and the mule ran away into the woods and threw him off his back. Then the mule kicked him in the head, stomped him and killed him.

About fifty years later James Harris, the uncle-in-law, moved into the house where this guy had lived. And Harris had a lot of mules.

Something took to disturbing his mules, and it happened almost every night. He would see a mule running around and around in the lot like someone was riding him. But he could never see anybody.

Then they thought that the man who had been killed might be coming back to worry the mules. So they tied a Bible to this mule and put him in the lot.

Then they'd go out there at night and see a little boy sitting on the rail fence around the mule lot looking like he wanted to get on a mule's back, but he never did. (P13).

—Jasper Porter.

Meaness Invites Evil Spirits (BA)

Our dog Tramp would never dig 'taters until we start. But one night a storm come up and Tramp was out there in the patch digging 'taters.

Papa look and when it lighten he say, "That Tramp." When it lighten again he shot and killed Tramp.

Then late one night another storm come up. We had a dog Rusty that was scared of lightning. Rusty came in the house and went under the bed.

"This girl tells her mama, "I'm scared; something in here; he's licking of me."

"What?" say her mother. "You do so much meaness in daytime you scared of everything . . . Old Bad Boy, ghosts and ha'nts . . . at night."

They struck a light. They opened the door and ran Rusty out. (L3).

—Mrs. Harvey Lassiter.

'Mother' Drives Out Demons (BA-J)

"My aunt who lives in Boykins, Virginia, but was raised eight miles out in the country near Nat Turner's cave, told me about this woman who could drive out demons," said an eleven-year-old.

This woman knew how to make the spirits do things. And people called her *Mother*. And there was this man who was rolling in all kinds of sin, and he wanted to do better. Someone told him he should go to see Mother.

So this man went to see Mother. She prayed and said some strange words, then tapped him on the head and shoulder, one time, two time, three time.

When she tapped him three time this man fell out, he fell to the floor foaming at the mouth. The demons rolled out of him, rolled out with the foam of his mouth.

After that this man didn't drink whiskey, and he didn't do anything bad. (J13).

—*McCoy Jordan.*

Catches the Devil (WA)

"When I was a right large boy," said an ardent fisherman, "I slipped off fishing one Sunday instead of going to church with the rest of the family. When I got home my mother scolded me and told me what I had done was downright dangerous.

When she was a child her grandfather told her the story of a man who went fishing every Sunday, refusing to heed the warnings of his family and friends that he might meet with ill fortune.

'Then one Sunday he pulled up a ball of fire . . .'

"Nonsense!" he would tell them and keep right on breaking the Sabbath.

Then one Sunday he pulled up a ball of fire, and he saw a little horned man inside. He dropped his fishing pole and ran home frightened almost out of his senses.

He was certain that the Devil had put a curse on him, and when his folks came home from church they found him stretched out on a table.

Each Sunday thereafter he got on the table, stretched out and lay there until sundown . . . doing penitence for his abuse of the Lord's day.

And when people asked him why he no longer went fishing on Sunday he would reply, "If you pulled up a ball of fire like I did, you'd never go fishing on Sunday." (B21).

—Herbert Burgess.

Too Hot for the Devil (WA)

One time a man and the Devil made a bargain. They were to sit on a red hot stove. If the man sat longer, the Devil would make him rich; if he did not, the Devil would get his soul.

After awhile the man began squirming around and the Devil asked what was the matter. The man said he was looking for a hot place. The Devil jumped up and said, "I done burnt my tail."

So the man was rich the rest of his life. (G8).

—Louis Griffith.

16.
Spirits of Forbidding Places

Survival of the Fairies

Although tales of fairies, brownies and other sprites were extremely popular in Mother England and other European countries from 1700 to 1850 these supernaturals did not fare too well in the New World. It was not that they were not liked, but because the more scary spirits were more popular.

Those *little people* who have survived retired to desolate and rugged places and sometimes keep the hours of ghosts and infernal spirits.

In white folklore they still frequent the grassy wastes of the Great Dismal Swamp, like Paradise Old Fields and the Green Sea. Those places were filled with grottos, old timers said, and the spirits traveled underground passages from them to beautiful and mysterious Lake Drummond.

Although the fairy clan is virtually unknown in black folklore descendants of the old slaves in Gates County report that they lived in the deep woods and came forth at night to steal a human baby from its cradle and replace it with a fairy one.

As fallen angels, in Hertford County, fairies still go about at night playing beautiful music. But to assure themselves survival they have changed themselves into ghostly beings.

A few hundred yards from old Pitch Landing on Chinquapin Creek is an old cemetery. Years ago

He looked into the eyes of a blue-eyed rabbit.

a group of young people were walking home from a party long after midnight. As they approached the long abandoned creek landing they heard the strains of music which seemed to be coming from the creek swamp. It moved at a brisk pace from the forest into an open field. Under the pale moonlight the astonished merrymakers saw a group of small musicians dressed in white move over the cemetery and there with their music disappear. (M7).

Some of the gentle stories were made witchy. A salesman of Ahoskie, North Carolina, had his car to break down some distance from a garage but near the home of a widow whom he had heard people at the country stores say practiced witchcraft. Nonetheless he went to this home to phone for help.

No one answered his knock immediately. But he was astonished as he looked into the eyes of a blue-eyed rabbit about three or four feet high. The creature with human features peered at him from a corner of the house. The rabbit disappeared and moments later a beautiful young woman answered the door.

Not long after that he heard that the woman had been found dead in her home from gunshot wounds.

A local farmer said that he feared he had slain her. A strange creature had been disturbing his livestock. He suspected it was a witch and shot it with a load of silver. (M7).

The Spirit of the Pocosin (WA)

Diabolical agents found themselves as comfortably at home in the North Carolina swamps, pocosins and marshes as they had years earlier in the English bogs and moors.

The evil Jack-o'-lantern, the frightful Plat-Eye and various mysterious spirits, upon nightfall, took complete possession of such places. Even the horseback rider had cause for a choked throat while passing through dark forests in the dark of the moon or when the moon darted behind a cloud. For a being similar to the English and Scotch *Silkie* lurked in the dark woods ready to jump up behind him.

In the depths of the great pocosin, places unexplored by man, lurked hostile and deadly spirits. From one such place in Martin County comes the story of the untimely fate of a man who sought to penetrate its deep mysteries.

—o—

Before the Englishman Morant, only one serious attempt to penetrate the Dark House Pocosin had been made—an unsuccessful one. The pocosin, dense and impenetrable, lay deep in the West Dismal Swamp between Washington and Jamesville. After the English lumber company abandoned its expedition, Morant, a surveyor, determined to head a party into the middle of the pocosin.

But he could not attempt it alone. None of the guides or lumber cruisers would accompany him. His neighborhood friends refused to go. On every hand he was admonished to respect the *Spirit of the Pocosin*.

Finally Morant gathered a pitifully small party of protesting men. Equipped with everything the surveyor considered necessary, the men met to begin the venture. Morant was eager and confident. His plan was to follow a woodland path until it became indiscernible, then push forward through the middle of the pocosin to Diamond City and the sawmill on the other side of the Dismal.

The party waved to neighbors, who watched incredulously, and set off down the path. At first they walked easily, winding among the trees and dodging fallen limbs. Morant seemed to enjoy the coolness of the swamp and the slosh of mud beneath his boots. He drew up to his full height and breathed deeply.

On and on they walked, led by Morant with his compass and tripod. The men followed, joking and talking roughly. Gradually the way became difficult. The track dwindled, then disappeared. The underbrush thickened, and the growth became full of moving, crawling things. All about were pools of inky black water which emitted a peculiar, pungent odor.

Morant began to slow. He walked without speaking as he and his followers fought their way through the darkening swamp. The only sound was the *slush-slush* of the mud and the breaking of brush.

After a time, ominous stillness came. The atmosphere no longer cooled and refreshed. A dense opressiveness closed in on Morant and his party. Leaves hung motionless. The odor of stagnant water was heavy on the air. Vines twined about the tree trunks. Several times the growth seemed impenetrable.

The men grew restless. They looked from side to side, muttering to themselves. Even Morant seemed uncomfortable. But he was now doubly bent on conquering the Dark House Pocosin.

Snap! The blade broke as the huskiest of the men attempted to cut his way between two trees. He threw the knife into the brush and turned.

"This is enough," he said. "Are we to be swallowed alive in this black hell? I, for one, am ready to quit and go back."

Then there was confusion, everyone talking at the same time.

"Silence," shouted Morant, and they grudgingly gave him their attention. "Control yourselves! Are we to act like women because of a few bushes?"

"Women indeed!" retorted one. "Men, we would be fools to attempt to go further."

"I have a wife and baby," said another. "The risk is too great."

Morant was exasperated. He threatened, he pleaded, he argued, but to no avail. The men were determined. Finally he gave up. "All right," he said. "I will go on alone." He would not heed the warnings. "Stay here, and I will return by three o'clock," he said, and plunged alone into the swamp.

Noon came, but there was no sunshine, no light, only the same oppressive dampness. They tried to sing and joke, but after a few half-hearted attempts, fell into silence which seemed unendurable. A wild bird screamed from a tree, startling them, and a black snake slithered into a dark pool.

After what seemed an eternity, three o'clock came, then four. They yelled, but no sound came, not even an echo. Their very voices seemed swallowed in the blackness. They became panicky and decided to search for Morant. They tried to follow his trail of broken branches and underbrush, but without success. Minutes dragged and still they could find no trace. The swamp was like a grim, silent man, who tells nothing. Then they heard a shout, "My god, come quickly!"

They pressed forward in the direction of the voice, stumbling, falling, tearing their faces and bodies on thorns and brush. Finally they reached a small clearing and stopped, staring with horror at the dead body of Morant. The arms and face of the dead man were scratched and torn like theirs, but around his neck

'My God come quickly!'

was a ring of bruised and broken places as if he had been choked to death They stood silent, paralyzed.

Then in silent panic they fled in the direction of home. No sound hindered; no obstruction stayed them. Silent, speechless, dumb with fear, for hours, on and on they pressed until they reached the clearing.

Next morning, guiding a rescue party, they went back for Morant's body. They reached the point where Morant had left them. Later they agreed they had found the spot where his dead body lay, but no body was there, nor any trace of it.

The land company declined and failed, and people forgot the Dismal and its Dark House Pocosin. The railroad was abandoned, and Diamond City became a ghost town. (V8).

(The story was told to W. L. Vaughan by S. F. Freeman who as a boy worked at Diamond City Sawmill.)

The Lowry Hideout (AI)

I can't remember the man's name; but he was a Lumbee Indian who lives in Robeson County between Pembroke and Maxton; and he told me this while we were returning from South Boston, Virginia, where we had gone to look at some equipment for the Evans Crossing Fire Department.

This man had gone hunting in a large and wild swamp, and I think it was Raft Swamp. After considerable wandering he was looking for a landmark, and he sighted a large tree a short distance ahead. It was so large that he drew close to examine it, to beat on it to see if it was hollow. To his surprise he saw that it had been hollowed out and fitted with a door just big enought to admit a large man. A hole had been bored through the door and through this passed a chain, and the chain was secured with an old and rusty padlock. It looked to be a hundred or more years old.

He beat on the tree and it boomed hollow. The Lowry outlaws had hidden out in these wilds, he recalled, and he thought perhaps this had been one of their hideouts.

So he didn't tell a soul about it; and he said to himself, "This is going to be mine whatever is in there." So he went home and returned with a crow bar with which to pry open the door and a toe sack to carry away whatever loot that might be found.

But his efforts went for naught; he couldn't get in; every time he tried to pry the door open something would come up from behind and grab him and throw him into creek.

Convinced he couldn't open the door alone he returned home and asked several friends to go with him. They laughed at him but finally went along to humor him. But this time he could not find the tree. Perhaps he will chance upon it again, he hopes. (H1).

—*A. C. Hall, Jr.*

The Jack-O'-lantern

The Jack-o'-lantern, sometimes known as Jack-of-the-lantern, will-o'-wisp, Peg-a-lantern, Kitty-candlestick, and Jacket-a-wad, is the most common light among southern blacks but is given little notice by the whites. It retained characteristics similar to Old World lights.

The Scotch believe in the will-o'-wisp, and in Ayrshire there is a rhyme to remind the children that the light bearer is a demon:

Spunky, Spunky, ye're a jumping light,
Ye ne'er tak hame the school weans right;
But through moss, and owre the hag,
Ye drown the ill anes in your watery den!
(P17, p. 134).

Thus, beware little ones lest Spunky leads you to a watery grave.

Meanwhile in the west of England the Pigseys in human form and carrying lanterns were seeking to lead the unwary into bogs. Their power could be broken by wearing one's coat wrong side outwards.

Late in the eighteenth century a demon was frequenting the deep swamps of North Carolina and Virginia, and it came to be known at the Jack-o'-lantern. It appears in the piedmont and mountain areas early in the nineteenth century. By now the *jack-mer-lantern* had acquired a secure footing among the whites of Surry County, North Carolina. (B13, pp. 269, 271).

One Uncle Billy came upon the chain jingling demon upon a dark and drizzly night, causing him to shoot at a neighbor's horse instead of a deer. He had to hide in a mud pond from men who came to see about the horse. Afterwards the ugly thing stood grinning at him as he struggled to get out. (B13, p. 171).

Old Jack came to be feared almost as much as the Devil. Thus he was able to compete with him for interest and attention. At the opening of the twentieth century he had acquired an important place in the southern black folk tradition. It was contended that once the Jack-o'-lantern had cast his spell a person must follow him into thickets, swamps, and pocosins to possible death.

Thus if one should see a floating light in a nearby swamp, "turn your back on it and go home as fast as you can." (P6, p. 206). To break the demon's spell one should turn his pockets wrong side out, turn his hat or cap backwards, and fall down on his face; (D2) or he might carry a knife that had never cut wood. (D1, p. 248).

Although Jack usually is represented in the form of a man, in some localities he possesses special characteristics. In parts of the south he is "a hideous creature five feet in height, with goggle-eyes and huge mouth, its body covered with long hair," which bounds through the air like a giant grasshopper. In this frightful form he is stronger than a man and swifter than a horse. (S5, p. 18).

Various legends, chiefly among southern blacks, tell how Jack was transformed from a man into a frightful demon. (J7, pp. 121-126).

Most follow a general theme, but vary as to details, being more or less adapted to the locale in which they are found. In all, while an evil man on earth, Jack has some unsatisfactory dealings with the Devil. Jack causes the Devil so much trouble that when he seeks to enter hell he is rejected. The Devil explains that already he has caused him too much trouble and wishes to have nothing more to do with him. Those in charge of heaven having already turned him down, Jack finds himself with no place to go. So as a last accomodation, the Devil gives him a glowing ember from his fiery pit to light his way through eternal darkness.

In a white version, the Devil tells him, "Go and make yourself a hell of your own." (C1). In others, Jack returns to earth with his fireball and stumbles about the swamps and other dark places.

Always he is seeking to lead people into disaster.

The Plat-Eye

When the new moon is pale and yellow and the shades of night drawn choking tight one should avoid the borders of the great swamps and pocosins and lonely wooded paths.

From far back in slavery times this has been the time of the dreaded *Plat-Eye*, the frightful spectre which has driven countless people out of their senses.

It has been seen in many forms throughout the southern states. Usually it appears in the form of some animal, often as a little dog with fiery eyes. But at times it may be of monstrous size, like coming of a large horse with heavy hoof-beats, which shifts its form to that of a little dog. It may come out of a dense and forbidding swamp or pocosin as a low hung cloud and envelop its victim. (P17, p. 131). And should one hit at it it may increase to enormous size.

The Nat Turner Plat-Eye (BA)

After his execution in 1831, Nat Turner of Southampton County, Virginia, returned in several spirit forms. In one he was a dreaded plat-eye.

In a branch near the home of his slain master, Joseph Travis, he might appear "like a bull cow with long horns and breathing fire and smoke; and again he might be like a large Shepherd dog. If one popped a horse whip at him "his eyes turn red as fire. One man left that *dog* alone, but one night his mule accidentally hit the spirit. Whereupon he "got big as a cow . . . had legs on 'im . . . eyes just as red as a coal of fire . . . eyes big an' shiny . . ." (J5, p. 185).

The Log (WA)

Many years ago, three-quarters of a century or more, W. E. Vann was a boy living in a rural Hertford County community. A swamp with a small stream passed through this community, and there was considerable passing along the puncheoned roadway and its footway and footlog which linked the many farms on each side of it.

Many years earlier, old folks said, a man of the area had disappeared; and not long afterwards his body was found in the swamp near the crossing. He had been murdered, it was supposed; but his murderer never was discovered. The mystery was a topic of discussion for many years. Then strange things began to happen at the crossing, and some people said the ghost of the dead man was frequenting the place.

At twilight or deeper into the night a headless dog, or a racing white horse had been seen, and some had been engulfed in a hot and clammy body of air. The boy heard many such tales.

Then night caught him on the side of the swamp opposite his home. There was no other crossing than the haunted one. So he choked back his fears.

As he approached the shadowy place he sensed danger. The air was still and clammy, and the roadway narrowed and trees hugged in close to shut out the light from the sky.

About midway something like a headless dog came from an inky hiding place into the faint light. Then it drifted nearer while uttering a low threatening growl. He picked up a stick and when very near he struck at it. But there was no blow; instead, the stick passed through the form as nothing were there; and instantly the thing disappeared.

Next day the boy returned through the swamp.

Where he had cast aside the stick there lay a log, one so large that he could not lift one end of it. The log looked strange, it was old and mossy, but it could not have been there before, one couldn't miss seeing it.

A few days after that the boy passed the same way again, and again he was astonished, the old log was gone. Not even a print of it remained in the soft mud. (V1).

—Linwood Earl Vann.

The Growing Ha'nt (BA)

The Plat-Eye often appears in folk tales as it does in this instance:

These two men were going through the country in a wagon. As night approached they saw no house at which to call and beg for lodging. It was getting dark as they came upon an old abandoned house. This would provide better shelter than the open sky, they agreed, so they stopped.

One of the men built a fire in the fireplace and was cooking their supper while the other sat by talking and waiting. Then something scratched a little soot down in the frying pan.

"Where in the hell did that soot come from?" cried the man attending the frying pan.

Before his companion could answer something like a cat leaped down from the chimney and went and sat in a corner of the room. The man left his pan on the fire and went over and kicked at the *cat* thing to run him out of the house.

Instead of running, the thing started growing. First it was like a dog, then as big as a hog, then a calf, and finally a horse.

When like a horse the thing set on the man who cursed, and his partner ran for his life. He never did go back to the old house, but he said he thought the thing took his companion away.

This man who got away doesn't stop at old houses any more. (B10).

—*Edward Beverly*

The Frog and the Grave Diggers (BA)

"That was the last grave I ever dug," said Horace Futrell, gravedigger, "and I ain't got no plans for digging another one."

Until about twenty years ago Horace worked full time for an undertaker. He didn't find anything objectionable with his work until one foggy and misty morning:

"We had dug this grave as deep as we were going and were spading down the sides when a frog jumped in. And I just slipped my shovel under him and threw him out. A heavy fog came over the grave, and I looked and there was the frog in there again. He acted queer; his eyes were bigger than any frog I had ever seen, and they flashed red flashes. I threw him out with my shovel . . . way over. But here come that little cloud, and there was the frog back in the grave.

"John Eley and Lijah Barnes were working with me, and they took up the frog and carried him way back in the woods, I'd say about half a mile. Before they got back here come that little cloud, and there was that frog in the grave puffed up big as two, three, four frogs . . . eyes flashing.

"We hurried on through and left that frog. If he

wanted that grave, as far as we were concerned he could have it!

"I told my boss man I was quitting when I heard folks say it had thundered during the funeral." (F7).

—*Horace Futrell.*

The Sooey Ghost (BA)

About eleven o'clock one night this man was walking along a narrow way in Bertie Connty's Indian Woods. Zig-zag rail fences followed close beside each side of the primitive earthen way.

Overhead a new moon darted in and out behind wind-swept mares' tails throwing scraggly shadows over the fields and wooded branches and bogs.

As the playful shadows flitted overhead the man came up on a *sooey*, or sow ghost, a demon-like being, with a drove of little pigs, little demons, behind her. Quickly he saw she was no ordinary hog. "The sow . . . ghost . . . was slick on this side and black on the other . . . red eye on this side and black eye on the other . . . great long *tusches* . . . little pigs coming out of the fence locks and going back into others.

"That sow . . . ghost . . . came up to me and opened her mouth . . . groaned, *O-o-o-m,* and disappeared in the fence lock.

"I tell you here and I tell you now, this nigger got away from there; he know what that slick side and red eye mean." (S6).

—*Noah Smallwood.*

17.
Magic and Miscellaneous

The Magic of Boaz Squires (WA)

Some time before the Revolution one Boaz Squires came to North Carolina and settled between the Neuse and Pamlico rivers at a place later to be known as Alliance in Pamlico County.

Squires must have come from Scotland, for he brought with him a power of wizardry equal to that of the famed Scotch folk figure Michael Scott.

It so fell out that upon a trip to Edinburgh Scott came upon and slew a large white serpent. After relaxing at the next public-house the landlady was told of his exploits. This woman, gifted in the *arts* had the mid portion of the snake fetched. It was still quivering with life. Through a keyhole in his door Michael saw her place the portion in an oven with other ingredients and afterwards extract it and place it for cooling on the hearthplace. At an opportune time he emerged from his quarters, dipped his finger in the sauce and applied it to the tip of his tongue. Whereupon the cock crowed and the landlady was obliged to divulge to him a knowledge of the remainder of her secrets. Thus the Scotchman was endowed with the knowledge of *good and evil* and all the *second sights* that might be acquired. With such powers he "seduced some thousands of Satan's best workmen into his employment," and it was through their supernatural energies that many monumental architectural works were constructed.

It so seems that our Boaz Squires as a young man acquired like powers over the helpers of Satan before he sat out to make a place for himself in the New World.

His new neighbors were fishermen, turpentine and tar producers, and livestock raisers. Their products were moved to nearby and foreign markets by boats, canoes, periguars, flats and ships of various kinds and sizes. So Squires decided that he should apply his peculiar advantages to boat building.

A farmer, a fisherman or a woodsman could place his requirements before Squires and have the finished craft in prompt order. This promptness together with the unexcelled quality of the product led to curiosity among his neighbors. Squires did not object to divulging the knowledge that he possessed supernatural powers; it was the *art* of their application which he carefully guarded.

It was told by these same neighbors that he was so sure of his strength that he did not shrink from engaging the Devil in a battle of fistics. Sometimes when Squires sat at his supper table something would come knocking on his door; he was called out; and in the shadows of night the sound of blows were heard. Squires always returned *dusting off his hands,* signifying he had been the victor.

When Squires wished to build a boat, it was said, he would go into the woods with axes and lay them at the foot of trees which were to be used. Other necessary tools were placed about. He retired to whatever leisure he desired while his demons worked through the day for him.

One time he was given an urgent order, and the boat

was produced in one-half a day. At mid-morning there came the sound of felling of a great tree in the forest, then the knocking and hammering like many men at work. At noon when the people went to the river to witness the launching Squires was sitting upon the craft softly whistling.

Now, Squires had brought with him from the Old World an old black trunk which he would permit no one to open. But eventually his wife's curiosity got the best of her. She cracked open the trunk lid to peep in, and out came two demons in the form of black cats. Squires died immediately. He was laid to rest at the old Jim Tingle homeplace at present Alliance. Yet some say he is not at rest. Most mornings, especially in fall, a misty cloud boils into strange shapes as it rises from his grave. Some fear that the unleased demons are after their former master. (S14, pp. 83-84; J7, pp. 103, 105).

The Whistling Snake (BA)

"Mighty nigh everybody has seen a *hissing snake,* but that ain't the kind I'm talking about; I say he was a *whistling snake,* and I say he the only snake that whistles that I have ever heard of." Betty Jane Futrell was telling her grandchildren about the time when she was a girl and a slave on the Walter Futrell plantation in Northampton County, North Carolina.

"Folks was out there chopping cottton, most everybody, the grass was some kind of bad. You know we sing, most of us sing or hum, and a man might whistle.

"This day we alls is singing, 'cept somebody is whistling, but we look and everybody is singing, but there is this whistling. We stop and the whistling stops. We starts and the whistling starts . . . real sharp, purtiest whistling you ever did hear, coming up out of the ground all about out feet.

"We quit, it quits.

"We get to the end at the woods. Sis Lulu sits down on a log to get her breath, and the *log* starts crawling away with her. She jumps up screaming, we look, we see it's a big snake. We scared to death. That snake, he follow under our feet across the field!"

The hoe hands, said Betty Jane, ran from the field and would not return. But Master Futrell knew a group of Indians who lived about two or three miles away on Potecasi Creek. (According to tradition, in the 1830's several Indian families were living on Potecasi Creek about two miles east of N. C. Highway 11.) Fortunately one old man among them professed to understand the workings of the supernatural. The *whistling snake* was a monster and the work of the Devil, the old Indian explained, and "Marster Futrell pay him to get shut of it." The grass grew unhindered until after the old man had gone around the field sprinkling a strange powder and chanting a strange ritual.

"That fix the *whistling snake*," asserted Betty Jane; "he didn't get in the field no more." (M10).

—*Dallas Moore.*

Indian Snake Tales (AI)

The Indian regarded the snake the work of their Evil Spirit, equivalent of the Christian Devil, and a feared enemy. The Tuscaroras of the North Carolina coastal plains had many tales of monster snakes. Lawson says that the Indians avoided killing a snake for fear that "some of the Serpents Kindred would kill some of the Savages' Relations." (L2, p. 223).

One snake tale, says Lawson, was about "a great Rattle Snake, which, a great while ago, lived by a Creek in that River, which was Neus, and that it killed abundance of Indians; but at last a bald Eagle killed it and they were rid of a Serpent that used to devour whole Canoes full of Indians at a time." (L2, p. 226).

Running From the Devil (BA)

"You gotta watch out for dat *Old Villian*. He might catch you and take you away to his *Nest*." Horace House, born a slave near Margarettsville, North Carolina, would warn his grandchildren in the 1920's as he rounded out more than eighty years in the home of a daughter in Newsoms, Virginia.

One of the grandcildren is Susie Mae Brooks. She explains that the Old Villian was the old man's Devil, and his nest was his hell.

At times Old Horace would sing a song which he said soon after the Civil War he had heard sung by spirits of sinners buried in Old Zion Church cemetery. He learned it from them one eventful night.

While passing by the church he saw it all lighted up and heard something like folks singing. It wasn't time for a revival or a prayer meeting, and thinking some special event was being held, Horace decided to attend. As he turned off the country road and entered the church grounds he made out these words:

> *Fire in the east,*
> *Fire in the west,*
>   *I'm running from fiah;*
>   *Running from the Villian's Nest;*
>   *I'm running from fiah.*
>
> *Fire in the north,*
> *Fire in the south,*
>   *I'm running from fiah;*
>   *Running from the Villian's Nest;*
>   *I'm running from fiah.*
>
> *Fire on the earth,*
> *Fire in the sky,*
>   *I'm running from fiah;*
>   *Running from the Villian's Nest;*
>   *I'm running from fiah.*
>
> *Fire up here and*
> *Fire down below,*
>   *Fiah, fiah everywhere;*
>   *Running from the Villian's Nest;*
>   *I'm running from fiah.*

" 'Never hear any singing like that befo' . . . and I ain't hear none since. Like folks scared about to death!' my grandpa say. And then he say, 'In them days I don't have nothing agin a little brandy; but I tell you here and I tell you now, that night I ain't drunk a drap.'

"My grandpa say he goes on up to the church door, and just as soon as he gets there all the lights go out and the singing stops. He looks inside and he don't see nobody, and then he starts to go away, and before he gets back to the road the lights go on, the music and the singing start up.

" 'Tell you here and I tell you now,' say my grandpa, 'I git away from dere; sound like spirits running from fire, I run like I running from fire, run six miles, run all de way home, fall flat on the floor, a long time before I can get enough breath to tell what happen.'

"My grandpa say his folks wouldn't believe him, 'my own folks! my own folks don't believe me!' But it ain't long before everybody know he is telling the truth. There was this family going by Old Zion one night; they see the church lit up and hear the singing going on. They think there is a prayer meeting, and they drive their cart up in the church yard. They don't see no carts and wagons there and they hear that *running from fiah* song. They whip their mule away from there, whip him down the road as fast as he can go, he is all lathered with sweat and about to drop when they git home."

Shortly after that one Wash Moore, a sinner-searing preacher, came down from Norfolk, Virginia, to conduct revival services. The reports of the singing sinner spirits reached his ears. He made a big stir over them; too many sinners were in the congregation as well as in the church cemetery. After he clomped about the stage with his boots chiming, *clip-lick, clip-lick, clip-lick* and he got the people to shouting he'd sing *Hide Me From My Angry God*, for *that dreadful day is coming by-m-bye*, verse after verse warning there would be no place to hide.

Shortly afterwards one might go by Old Zoin almost any night and see it lighted up and hear that singing. Prayer meeting attendance dropped off to a handful of the faithful. Something had to be done. Someone called on Bill Minton at his ramshackled home at Worrell's Mill in lower Southampton County near the North Carolina line. Minton claimed to have second sight and to be able to lay spirits.

Shortly afterwards small crosses made of the rattan vine, tree climber of the lowgrounds, were hanging over each window and each door of Old Zion. Quiet prevailed even upon the darker nights. Then one night the church burned down. Folks quickly laid the fire to the Seaboard train which ran near by; for it was in the habit of coughing out sparks and setting the woods afire all up and down its tracks.

With a few dollars from the good hearts of the railroad folks and a church raising, soon New Zion stood where Old Zion had stood.

And soon there were those same strange goings on in the new church.

And soon rattan crosses were hung at the new church.

And soon New Zion burned.

This time, "say Grandpa, by angry spirits of them sinners."

No new church was raised on the old site. But folks kept right on burying their dead in the old church cemetery.

"That place is some kind of ha'nted," explains Susie. "Dark nights you can see that graveyard full of little lights hopping about from place to place. Folks have seen them fly over to where the church stood and then wander back to the cemetery.

"Grandpa, he buried there," says Susie as if his folks had played a dirty trick on him. "And sometimes I thinks to myself, I thinks, 'Lawd have mercy, he must be having a worrisome time.'" (B17)

—*Susie Brooks.*

Sometimes an Imp appears in behalf of the Devil.

PART V
Portents and Omens

18.
Death Portents

DEATH PORTENTS must have arrived in the New World with each new group of English, Scotch and Irish immigrants. Here for many generations they competed with all kinds of supernaturals for their place in the lore of the fresh and ever changing land. And so were required to adapt their manners and appearances to the whims and fancies of the people.

Among the more interesting death portents one finds the *Wraith*, the *Banshee* and the *Barguest*. Of all the spectres the wraith seems to have undergone less change than most others. Perhaps this is because it is the supposed ghost of a person in his exact likeness which is seen shortly before or after his death.

In the Scotch highlands the wraith might enact the entire death drama in advance of the actual event— the death, the wake, the procession, the funeral services, and the burial. The ghostly actors would be exact duplications, or *yoke-fellows*, of the human ones, and they would perform each act in minute detail. (G4, pp. 16f).

Such beliefs came with the early arrivals. Late in the seventeenth century, says Cotton Mather, strange premonitions of approaching death "are such a frequent occurence in history that one is ready now to look upon them as no more than matters of common occurence." He then told of a wraith-like occurence in New England:

The Physician's Dream (WA)

For three nights in succession a physician neighbor saw his likeness in dreams, and he was miserably distressed to see this likeness being drowned. In the third dream "he was cast into extreme sweats, by struggling under the imaginary water."

He told his dreams to members of his family, and immediately two friends came and asked that he go a little ways with them in a boat.

At first he was afraid, but then he observed that the weather was so calm and asked himself, " 'Why should I mind my dreams, or distrust the divine providence?' " He went with his friends, but before night a thunderstorm struck suddenly and all three were drowned. (D5, pp. 161-162).

The Charlotte County Wraith (WA)

A story as fresh as one lifted directly from the Irish countryside a hundred years ago comes from Charlotte County, Virginia.

Midway the nineteenth century one John Duffer, a poor farmer of Irish descent, lived in Charlotte County. His farm was small, he owned no slaves, yet he fought for the Confederacy during the Civil War.

Poor John and his wife must have come from the Irish countryside. Familiar to them were many tales and beliefs that existed among Irish peasants at that time. John outlived his wife by many years, and he often told a story of her strange demise.

Late one morning, sun shining bright, while plowing a field Duffer looked and saw someone in the family cemetery.

"Who can that be?" Duffer wondered.

The furrow he was plowing took him nearby, and he recognized the graveyard visitor as his wife.

This was extremely odd, for it was time for her to be preparing his dinner.

Nonetheless, at the noon hour he unharnessed his mule and went to the house. To his surprise his dinner was on the table waiting for him.

"What were you doing in the graveyard there?" Duffer's curiosity prompted him to ask his wife.

"I haven't been in the graveyard," she replied astonished at his query.

"But I saw you there only a short while ago."

"Must have been someone else," she suggested.

"You're wrong, it was you, I saw you there, saw you very clearly," Duffer was positive.

Later that day Mrs. Duffer was taken very ill, and death came quickly. This caused her husband to have second thoughts. She had been an honest woman, and his accusation weighed on his mind. Upon which he began to relate his story to neighbors.

"I really didn't see Mary; it was a *doppleganger*." And a doppleganger to the Irish was much like the wraith in parts of Ireland, England and Scotland, a spectre which appears in the exact likeness of a person and so foretelling that person's imminent death. (M1).

—*William I. Marable.*

The Wraith of Watauga (WA)

From the North Carolina mountains comes the story of a doctor who had the misfortune to see his likeness.

For many years after the Civil War one Doctor Rivers lived at Boone and served the people of mountainous Watauga County for many miles about.

Sometimes a call, as often at night as during the day, would take him into the western part of the county through the Big Laurel. This was a jungle-like tangle of laurel ivy and all manner of scrub trees. Tales related by many people held that this was a sanctuary for unfriendly spirits.

It was in Big Laurel upon an eerie star-lit night that the Doctor learned of his own impending death. Between midnight and daybreak while returning from a call he came across a wraith or wraith-like apparition. "At a place where the road made a temporary bend to avoid a large fallen oak tree," says the informant, "the doctor was surprised to see in the road on the other side of the fallen tree a strange man sitting on a gray horse exactly like his own steed. Turning the bend into the main road the doctor was still worse surprised to find no horse nor man where he had just seen them. They seem to have vanished suddenly."

About two miles on his way the physician made a call at a farm house and told his story. He died a short time afterwards. Various acquaintances took the apparition of the likeness of the doctor and his horse to portend his approaching death. (B19, I, p.679).

The Death Warning (WA)

Little Boney Potter was a desperate character who lived in North Fork Township, Watauga County. He was killed in an encounter with a sheriff's posse.

A few nights before Potter's death his bedfellow was terrified by "something big and heavy (that) came and set down right on the bed." There it remained until shortly before daybreak, but Potter did not awaken.

After Potter's death his companion said that he was certain the strange visitor had foretold of his death. (G9, p. 31).

The Banshee or Banshide

As late as the nineteenth century, in England, Scotland and Ireland, the *Banshee was* regarded as a female fairy who attached herself to the better families—the castle folk—and this attachment required her to foretell the death of any member by wailing outside.

Her origin is obscure, but one Irish legend holds that once she was a beautiful maiden from the *Land of Youth*. Patrick Byrne, in his *Irish Ghost Stories*, says "such a one was Niamh of the Golden Hair who carried Oisin away with her." After years of persecution by the Danes and the English the fairy maiden was transformed into "a withered screeching hag" who combed her tousled hair with a broken comb. (B22, p. 38).

Yet accounts of her appearance vary from one locality to another. In one she might be "a very beautiful young girl with red hair, wearing a green kilt," in another, a bird with a human face, or as in Cornwall, a phantom tree, or as in Wales as "the dribbling hag." (S12, pp. 19-21). In the highlands of Scotland the Gabriel Hounds, flying beasts with human heads and animal bodies, served the same purpose. (H5, p. 98).

In most instances the banshee wrings her hands and utters a blood-curdling wail, which an elderly man described as a mournful sound which would have "put ye in mind of them old cats on the yard wall." A baker said he could make out one or two Gaelic words in her wail. (S12, p. 21).

There being no castles and few noble families on the American frontier, only a few of the banshee must have come to the New World with the peasant folks. Yet no less than one banshee came to North Carolina. Before the Revolution one such spectral lady of the pine barrens haunted the country along the Tar River a little below present Tarboro. She was a hardy as the grizzly human pioneers and a terror when compared to her kind in native Celtic countries.

One story of her extraordinary exploits has been handed down across two long centuries:

The Edgecombe Banshee (WA)

During the Revolutionary War some two hundred years ago one David Warner, an Englishman, ran a grist mill on the Tar River in Edgecombe County near present Tarboro.

As a staunch Whig a good part of the time he let his mill be used to grind wheat and corn for the rebels. The mill wheel turned steadily clattering from first morning light until coming of darkness. And at times the same monotonous clatter reached far into the night.

The English miller was "a big man with a shock of black hair and black beard whitened with flour dust. His eyes were keen as an eagle's, and there was a fierce strength in his arms and wrists. He could lift a sack of grain with one hand and fling it over his shoulders, and with one turn of his wrist he could snap a ten-penny nail in two."

It was May 1781 when the British crossed over the Tar River, at Duncan Lemmon's Ferry. Colonel Jethro Sumner wrote General Nath. Green, "The people are moving before them; most of the public stores here . . . will be moved off, and out of their way . . ." (NCSR, XXV, p. 456).

In the legend, when a Colonial horseman warned the miller of the enemy's approach he refused either to flee or to hide. "I'd rather stay and wring a British neck or two," he said grimly.

" 'But you can't stay and fight a whole army singlehanded.'

" 'Then I'll stay and be killed.' "

Warner was busy sacking meal when six soldiers arrived and found him to be an acknowleged Rebel. When they seized him and said that they were going to drown him in the river he laughed and jeered, " 'Go ahead, go ahead, but if ye throw me in the river, ye British buzzards, the Banshee will haunt ye the rest of your life, for the Banshee lives here.' "

Then the miller added, " 'When the moon is dark and the river's like black ink, and the mist is so thick ye can cut it with a knife, ye can see her with her yellow hair falling about her shoulders flitting from shore to shore, crying like a loon. And sure as the stars are in the sky, if ye drown me she'll get ye.' "

At first five of the men hesitated, wishing to wait for their commander, but a sixth said, " 'Why wait? We are sent on ahead to make the way safe.' "

'the mist took the form of a woman with a veil for her face.'

Three men seized the miller, weighted him with stones and threw him into the river. As his body sank "a piercing cry ripped from the red clay ledges—the cry of a woman in the agony of death . . .

"At first there was nothing save a thick mist above the water. Then the mist took the form of a woman with flowing hair and a veil for her face.

" 'The banshee,' whispered one soldier." Another chilly echoed the same. There was one with an evil eye and bloodier hands who without a word fled to the mill.

By nightfall the main British force arrived. Officers quartered in the mill house and their men camped beneath the trees. Then the new moon arose thin and yellow and a rain crow called from down the river. Then there came that same cry of a woman in the agony of death . . . a cry that brought officers from the mill house and men from their tents. But those three who had drowned the miller clasped their hands over their ears to shut out the wail.

A mist on the river took the "form of a woman with flowing hair and a veil over her face." Then no one was there, but far down the stream echoed the weird cry. It wailed, wailed . . . again and again.

The commander discovered the crime and decreed the three "for the rest of their lives should stay at the mill, grinding grain and listening to the haunting wail."

So they ground for the British by day and cringed at the wails of the banshee by night.

"Then one night the banshee came closer. She appeared in the doorway of the mill, a tall, mist-shrouded figure with flowing hair. She flung back her veil and faced the frightened men. The soldier with evil eyes cowed into the corner, but the other two leaped to their feet, lured by the misty apparition. The banshee floated away just beyond their reach. Blindly they followed. . . . They came to the river. There they stumbled, fell into the water and were never seen again."

The third soldier went raving mad. "All through the night he wandered the woods calling the miller's name. The cry of the banshee answered him. One day his body was found floating face upward in the very place where he had drowned the miller."

To this time — two long centuries — on an August night when the moon is right and the mist rises one may still hear the banshee cry — "an agonizing wail that rises higher and higher, beating against the distance where it fades away in a dull, throbbing moan." (S15).

The Dead Bells (WA)

Dead-bells, ringing in the ears, are particularly ominous in both Europe and America if they are loud, persistent and heard by two or more persons. A lady of Surry County, Virginia, tells of how she, her sister and their dying mother heard the bells:

"My mother had been in failing health for several years, and then time came when she began to weaken noticeably. One day, as I was about my house work, I heard a ringing noise. At first it seemed to be a dull faint ringing which I brushed aside as being only a ringing in my ears which would soon clear up as at times it had done in the past.

"But soon the ringing grew louder, and now it seemed to be coming from outside the house. I went out into the yard to see if I could learn what it was and where it was coming from. Now, it seemed to me it was like church bells ringing, ringing far away. What made it even more strange was that our neighbors had only farm bells, and our church, a mile or so away, had only one bell, and it was not the sound of this bell.

"At this time my sister came into the yard and asked me, 'Sis, do you hear that ringing?' And I told her that was what had brought me out of the house.

"When Sis and I found we could not learn from whence the ringing came we went back into the house. Our mother was glad to see us. She asked, 'Hear them bells . . . hear that beautiful ringing?' We told her we could. Then the ringing quickly faded away.

"Late the next day, as the evening sun sank low and a golden haze glowed about it the ringing came again. Mother had grown very weak and Sis and I, greatly concerned for her, were at her bedside. We heard her whisper weakly, almost silently, 'Hear the bells . . . hear . . . hear the bells . . . the bells are calling . . . call . . .'

"So Mother quietly passed away. Sis and I agreed that she heard the bells calling for her." (G3).

—*Miss Addie Goodrich.*

Old Wolf and the Fox (WA)

Years ago in the Gates County, North Carolina, community of Eure an Eskimo husky dog called *Wolf* earned an awesome reputation for himself before he died of old age.

Everyone knew that by tradition the mournful bark of a dog sometimes was a portent of the death of some loved one.

As Wolf advanced in years and earned the name of

Old Wolf folks began to notice that he possessed singular natural wisdom. Normally he was not noisy at night, but upon certain nights he would howl and howl as if endlessly mourning. Next day one could expect to hear that someone had died.

Year after year and time after time Old Wolf unfailingly announced almost every death of near and distant neighbors.

Announcement of Old Wolf's death also was a singular event.

A fox had frequented the woods and fields of Eure for many years. He was chased often by Old Wolf but never caught. Eventually folks said that both the dog and the fox were running just for the fun of it and had formed an extraordinary attachment one for the other.

One night the old fox was heard yapping near Old Wolf's home, but the dog didn't go out after him. Then he yapped and howled through the night.

Next morning the family found Old Wolf dead. (F1).
—*Billy Felton.*

The Screeching Owl (WA)

A spirit may become embodied as a screech owl and utter a chilling death warning.

Horton Cooper of Avery County, North Carolina, says to foretell this prophet of doom must come within a hundred feet of a home. And when a mountain woman of a few decades ago heard him she might sing,

> *When you hear the scrooch owl hollerin',*
> *Somebody's dyin', Honey,*
> *Somebody's dyin'.*   (C6, p. 73).

The Aerial Hound (WA)

About 1930 the people of rural Rowan County, settled chiefly by Scotch-Irish, occasionally were awakened at night by the eerie cries of a creature which ventured near their homes.

The thing, some explained, sounded like the wail of a human blended with the mourning howl of a dog.

But it was thought to be something other than a wild dog. For all the dogs cringed and ran for safety when it came about.

After awhile the people of a rural neighborhood between Salisbury and Hickory became very upset after hearing the cry for several nights.

When the thing approached one farm house the farmer was ready with his shotgun. This man slipped outside and hid in the shadows of some shade trees. In the moonlight, he said, he saw something the size of a big dog moving across the field towards him. He flicked off the gun's safety and prepared to fire. The thing seemed to hear the flick, which was too silent to disturb a hunted animal. It wheeled to one side, and the farmer saw that it was a being with a dog-like body and a human-like head.

The farmer was not surprised to hear next morning that a neighbor's wife had died during the night. At that he and various other people recalled that death of some acquaintance had occured each time the wail had been heard.

All were familiar with the belief that the howling of dogs was a portent of death and that in the Scotch lowlands the coming of the Gabriel Hound, a floating spectre with the body of a dog and head of a human sometimes announced it. (H1).

—A. C. Hall, Jr.

The Crowing Rooster (BA)

While there are death omens by the score in white and black folklore (C4, pp. 24-28; P17, pp. 82-83) one of the more interesting makes Chanticleer a prophet of death.

In the North Carolina mountains, "If a rooster turns his head outside the door and crows, the family will lose a member before the end of the year." (C6, p. 140).

In Northampton County upon the coastal plains, "If a rooster crows into the sunset, somebody in the family surely will die." (B7).

A few years ago Aunt Nick, an aged black woman, caught one of her roosters crowing at the setting sun. She got mad, went and took a stick and killed him. Then for several days she was miserable, lamenting to her daughter she might fall out at any time.

A few days afterwards a man came up the path to her home. She was frightened by the approach of this stranger, but she soon learned that he bore good news. Her sister in Norfolk, Virginia, had died.

After that Aunt Nick lamented the death of her best rooster; she said she felt downright wicked when he was not crowing for her at all. (B7).

The Falling Picture (WA)

A falling picture is one of the more common portents of death. A Bertie County, North Carolina, story illustrates how a person may be so marked for death.

Shortly after the Civil War Arie Rayner Lenow and her family were living in the old Ethridge house upon the west bank of the Chowan River near Colerain. The Ethridge family had moved elsewhere leaving the house furnished, including the family portraits hanging on the walls.

One night a violent storm swept over the countryside. Lightning flashed continuously and thunder jarred the house. Midway the storm the grandfather clock began striking while the hands were on neither the hour nor half-hour. Amidst the bonging Mr. Etheridge's picture quavered and then fell shattering to the floor, splattering the glass.

Next morning the news came, and it was not unexpected. Mr. Etheridge had died during the night and at the exact time his picture had fallen. (M9).

—Jimmy Moore.

PART VI
Ghosts, Ha'nts and Spectres

19.

Bridges to Eternity

THE itinerant preacher, armed with the Devil's pitch fork and the thunder of Providence, was but one step behind the first settlers of the North Carolina pine barrens and other remote parts. With such weapons he frightened black sinners into taking up salvation.

From then until the opening of the twentieth century one might hear another say that the saved die easily and that the unsaved suffer unspeakable agony.

Just a few years ago an old colored man, who had taken up the *yoke,* explained this manner of thinking: A sinner "sees hell before he gets there . . . sometimes snakes, spiders and other frightful things." These are the imps or little servants of the Devil, and they shoulder the duties of some Old World demons. Often the imps are seen at the death of a person, because they come to take the sinner's spirit away. (B10). A white informant explains that according to tradition "the marks of agony and despair" are left on the faces of the wicked dead. (A6).

Some blacks say that death attended by delirum is the result of witchcraft. (P17, p. 77). And if a person dies hard, he'll return and haunt the survivors. Thus every measure possible must be taken to help the afflicted pass into eternity as easily as possible. (P17, p. 81). To ease one's miseries during the morbid journey the person's head should be placed to the

•155•

east; but upon burial it should be placed to the west, into the setting sun.

For the saved, it seems, an inevitable hand reaches down to carry the souls to paradise. The death of *old saints,* aged pillows of the church, may be accompanied by a fiery display of lightning and drumming thunder. (A6). Some black folks say that the spirit of the saved "just goes to sleep" to await the day of Judgment, and there is no suffering. (B10).

The Guardian Angel (WA)

Belief in the *guardian angel* is found in America as early as 1638. At that time Father Edward Knott of Maryland told of how a licentious man repented of his evil ways and became godly. Once he was saved from drowning, and Providence interceded in his behalf and turned a terrible storm into another direction.

In time, after a long and good life, a Catholic attendant prayed at his death bed. An evil angel seemed to be present with diabolic intent. There also was a good angel present to prove his guardianship.

The priest heard the dying man say cheerfully, "Don't you see my good angel? Behold him standing near to carry me away; I must depart."

After this man's burial a very bright light often appeared around his tomb. (K2, p. 122).

The Death of Doctor Jim Jordan (BA)

A very religious Hertford County, North Carolina, conjure doctor, Doctor Jim Jordan, had a peaceful death in 1962. As he laid down his earthly burdens he seemed to be looking into paradise.

Shortly before, as his days grew fewer he expressed concern for his children. "Papa worried about us," says son Isaac; "he wanted to know how we were making out." He told his son Matthew, "It's alright with me. Has you got anything to eat?"

His minister and longtime friend dropped by to see him. The doctor told him, "If I don't see you any more, I expect to meet you at the Old Courthouse door." Thus he said in the words of the long-departed ex-slaves he expected to rejoin him before the Great Judge.

Saturday night and a few hours before death early Sunday morning, January 28, 1962, sister Jennie Mae was holding his hand. The weakening doctor knew:

"They're coming for me."

"Who're coming for you?"

"They're coming."

"Who're coming?"

"The Angels."

Later in a bare whisper the doctor mumbled: "I told you those people were coming; they're coming for me."

He just went to sleep slowly. He grew cold . . . his pulse beat a little . . . then there was none.

Doctor James Spurgeon Jordan was dead. (J4, pp. 132-133).

The Death of a River Runner (WA)

At times those who give little credit to the workings of the supernatural offer little or no contest to those who do. So did a young doctor more than a century ago.

It was soon after the Civil War. Young Doctor John Henry had completed medical school at Charleston, South Carolina, and was looking for a likely place to hang up his shingle. So about 1866 he moved into an old house two miles west of Beatty's Bridge in Bladen County, North Carolina. This was about twelve miles southwest of his old homeplace at Henry's Mill in Pender County near the Sampson line and well located to establish a medical practice in several communities along Black River in Bladen, Sampson and Pender counties.

This dwelling, which came to be known as the Brown Andrews place, was a compact story and a jump cottage which tradition said had been built before the Revolution. In more recent years it had served as the *great house* for a thriving plantation, but as the land wore out it was occupied by several undistinguished tenants.

The young doctor was warned he'd do well to look for another house, for ghosts had chased away several of its former occupants. He, however, lent only a curious ear to the tales of ghost antics. He moved in with his young wife.

After a few days the doctor heard strange noises, precisely like those he was warned he would. Immediately he set out in quest of the *ghost*. When he was inside the house the noise seemed to come from outside; and when he was outside it seemed to come from within. When he opened the door to go in or out the noise stopped. Then he looked through the keyhole of the large wooden lock to make sure there was no prankster. He saw the noise maker. This was but a small piece of paper which had lodged in the keyhole and fluttered when a draft forced air through.

—o—

Doctor Henry's shingle had not been out long before he was doing all the business that he could manage, but there was little pay in this war impoverished area other than chickens, ducks and farm produce. He was traveling up to ten miles in various directions, night and day . . . on horseback, by carriage and by boat.

It was not long after he had laid the ghost at his home before a four to five mile boat trip down Black River to Sandy Landing brought him into a second encounter with the supernatural, one he would remember to tell his grandchildren.

Old Gus, a former Henry family slave had elected to remain with his master after freedom and went with him on this call. Gus laid himself to the oars, and their dugout boat delivered them to the sick man's place much quicker than would have been possible by horse and carriage.

All of Gus' work was not menial. He was an able assistant, the doctor said he was better than any midwife he had ever known.

They climbed the river hill at Sandy Landing and proceeded to a one-room river shack where they found one Lunch Brown alone and burning with typhoid fever, already in delirium.

Little they could do other than await the afflicted's journey into death.

Brown, a longtime raft runner and in recent years a boat pilot, was a rude man as was some of the river runners. Addicted to booze, most of his meagre pay bought whatever joy it might provide. His impoverished family, reduced to desperation, had left him.

A few weeks earlier a man had been lost overboard from a steamboat that Lunch was piloting through the river's Narrows. He was one Roosevelt, also a boozer, who got too intoxicated, lost his footing and fell into the path of the steamer's paddles.

Now, while Lunch was dying Gus worked beside the doctor. He kept the sweat wiped from his face with a damp cloth. At times the patient seemed to be fleeing in terror from snakes, spiders and other terrifying creatures. Then he paused, gasped, lashed out his arms and cried, "It's hot . . . hot . . . hot as hell up here. Look out down there, Roosevelt, here I come!" His frame grew limp; the doctor searched for a heart beat and then pressed his eye lids and his gaping mouth shut.

Night was falling as Gus oared their boat upriver. At first both he and the doctor kept sober silence; but then Gus spoke up, "Boss, I believe that man seed his hell."

"Maybe." Doctor Henry didn't take pains to dispute.

As the bordering swamps darkened two or more owls commenced a noisy conversation, and Gus listened to them attentively as if trying to detect anything unusual in their tones.

Then there came a long and drawn out rumbling from downriver. The doctor supposed, "Somebody must be dynamiting."

Gus looked up into the clear sky, and said, "It ain't dynamite and it ain't thunder. Must be the Devil upping his voice and coming for Mr. Brown."

The doctor didn't dispute Gus on this point either. (J12; C8).

—*Nolon Johnson and*
Evelyn Johnson (Mrs. Hill) Corbett.

The Wire to Heaven (BA)

"I am sure my grandaddy, Cam Futrell, saw paradise on his deathbed," says a grandson.

The old man lived in Milwaukee, Northampton County. He was very religious and talked about the

Scriptures upon every opportunity. He was certain he would go to heaven after death.

Cam grew to be very old and very saintly. But in time he grew tired, worn out and mostly confined to his bed.

"One night, my mother who was attending him looked out of the window and saw the nearby cemetery lit up bright . . . from a light cricling overhead." Then it fell to the ground and left everything in darkness.

" 'I knew then my father's time on earth would not not be long,' said my mother. And next day Granddaddy grew much worse, so much that relatives were called to his bedside. As he was dying my mother and others heard him say, " 'Reach over there and touch that wire from my bed to heaven.' " (M10).

—Dallas Moore.

The Death of a Spinster (WA)

Occasionally one finds the belief that a person dies easier in his or her own bed or home. Oscar Lane of Whaleyville, Virginia, tells a story that supports this:

It was midway the 1930s, and Old Lady Becky Woofrey, a tall and withered white haired spinster, was on her death bed. Until taken with her mortal illness for many years she had lived alone in the old Woofrey home one mile north of Merchant's Mill in Gates County. Now, over her protests, she was at her brother's home about a mile south of the old mill. She was distressed at having to spend her last days in a strange bed.

The Woofrey family had prospered before the Civil

War, and afterwards it grew poor and broke up. But Miss Becky lived on at the old place, hoping to find the family treasure, which was said to have been hidden from the Yankees when she was a small girl and never recovered.

People of the neighborhood visited the brother's home to cheer up Miss Becky. Among these were Oscar Lane and his wife. Their way took their mule and cart by the old Woofrey place.

Upon their return it was late at night and dark, so dark that they had to let their mule keep the way. As they passed the Woofrey house it was completely swallowed up by darkness . . . and stillness.

But as they neared the picket fence gate a pitiful cry rang out from the place, a cry precisely like that of Miss Becky: "Oh Lord, help me . . . I'm so bad off!" After a deadening silence the plea was repeated louder than before.

"Whoa!" Lane pulled up the mule and handed the lines over to his wife.

She pushed them back at him and commanded through gritted teeth, "Don't stop here! Drive on, drive on!"

Lane slapped the mule with the lines, and as they trotted away he thought he heard Miss Becky still calling, "Help me, Mr. Lane. H-e-e-l-l-p . . ."

Next day word was passed through the neighborhood that Miss Becky had died the night before; and the Lanes learned that her death came but a short time after they had left her at her brother's home . . . and when they were passing her old home.

Soon some people of the neighborhood observed that peace no longer rested over the old Woofrey home. Several tenant families moved in and quickly moved out. William Ducks and his family were the last. Ducks reported that on their first night they heard "chains clanking down the stairway." They already were uneasy and didn't wait to investigate. They ran to a neighbor's home to finish out the night. They left the community without returning to the old place for their belongings. Ducks left no forwarding address for the hants to latch onto.

Now, completely without care, grass and shrubs and vines reached up from the earth and pulled a veil over the mysterious doings at the old place while the heavens poured out rain and rot.

Several years afterwards the ruins were removed to make way for farm land.

And in the ruins the family treasure was found . . . hundreds and hundreds of dollars which had been tucked away in a wall, possibly hidden by the grandfather who had donned the grey and honored the Woofrey name under Lee.

But the treasure was in Confederate dollars, Confederate currency . . . a big hand full of worthlessness.

Money gone, all leveled except a crumbling chimney and crumbling stories of grandeur, the money ha'nt and whatever others there may have been let the place be. (L1).

—*Oscar Lane.*

Old Judge's Lament (WA)

A dog which is close to his master often seems to know when a misfortune befalls him and suffers grief.

This is the story of Judge, one such dog.

About the time of my father's retirement he obtained a German Shepherd puppy and gave him the name of Judge. They became inseparable companions,

Old Judge takes his place below master's window.

and the dog would follow Father wherever he went.

Years stretched out, and Judge, the onetime frisky puppy, became Old Judge. And the inevitable, the time for separation of master and dog, came.

Father grew old and feeble and was taken with a terminal illness which the doctors were able to delay for several years. Old Judge was miserable when his master was too ill to leave the house. It was then that Old Judge took up his resting place beneath his master's bedroom window. He seemed ever intent, listening to each and every sound within the house.

When his master grew gravely ill keeping up with the noises in the house seemed to be Old Judge's only interest. Then the final hour for his master neared; relatives gathered at the home; and as my father breathed his last Old Judge seemed to know. He lifted his head toward the window and uttered a long mournful howl; he howled and howled, again and again, until someone came with a friendly pat on the head and comfort.

Time took up anew. Days passed, but the familiar sounds in the master's room were now stilled. Soon the family observed that Old Judge himself seemed to be failing in health. Occasionally he would whimper, but his whimpers ever grew weaker and weaker. His loneliness soon came to an end; the family spaded a resting place for him at the back of the garden. (A6).

—*Robert Askew.*

20.

Messages from the Dead

THE belief that the dead has uncanny powers to communicate with the living is found amoung the early American settlers, and it was flourishing at the opening of the twentieth century. To this day there are occasions in which the dead seem to communicate with the living.

Near the end of the seventeenth century Cotton Mather said that apparitions after death "have been often seen in this land. Persons who had died abroad or at sea "within a day after their death, (have) been seen by their friends in their houses at home."

He cited an instance that came under his personal observation. On the morning of May 2, 1687, one Joseph Beacon "had a view of his brother, then at London." The apparition told of the brother's murder. In late June, about eight weeks later, news of the brother's murder arrived. It had happened at the time of the apparition. (M2, pp. 468-470).

Miss Julie's Return

About thirty years after the Civil War Mrs. Emily M. Backus of Saluda, North Carolina, had a collection of three antebellum Negro ghost stories published in *The Journal of American Folk Lore*. These, she said, was told to her by an aging black servant, Aunt Pattie.

Aunt Pattie would tuck her and the other white children up in a high feather bed; and before reclining on her palate, she would sit before the fire and relate ghostly tales to their terror.

She might say, "Some white folks done say dade folks done walk no more," and then proceed to spin tales of quite active *ha'nts*.

Opening one of her favorites she might say, "Blessed marster, it's been years next Tuesday week sence de great light come." It was about an hour before midnight when old master and mistress were returning from Colonel Pepper's where they had attended Miss Nannie's wedding. As their carriage drew near home they saw a light in every window of their great house.

" 'Lord a-mighty,' says old massa,' 'tis a fire!' " But when they alighted from their carriage and went into the house they found darkness everywhere. They looked everywhere but nothing seemed amiss.

But presently and all night long "somebody ware walking, walking up on the big stairs an' all over de house, an' it ware so for a week."

Those were terrible times, asserted Aunt Pattie. They were not the same as they had been. "Old massa never cracked no more jokes to nobody, an' ole missus looked white an' scared. Deytime all the folks goin' soft an' creepy like, an' every night dat awful walk."

Then one day old master got a letter from Ireland saying that Miss Julie who had married there was dead. After that letter there was no more light and no more walking.

"Dat ware Miss Julie come faster than de letter to de ole home," explained Aunt Pattie. Then she added, old mistress "think it Miss Julie ghost as I does." But old mistress didn't dare say so, " 'cause 'tain't religious, she say, to talk such." (B1, p. 228).

•167•

The image was 'a light bulb with my father's face'

A Message From Her Father

Mrs. Dorothy Hand Wagoner tells of receiving a strange death notice at her home in Gates County on December 8, 1964.

Her father was seriously ill in Louise Obici Hospital in Suffolk, Virginia; and her brother, Doctor Leroy Hand, had ordered her to bed with an injured leg. She suffered such discomfort that she was long in going to sleep, but then deep slumber came.

In the early morning hours "I was suddenly awakened from that deep sleep; and I realized that I had been awakened by a bright image, an instantaneous thing far removed from any type of dream. And the image that I saw was a light bulb with my father's face in it. It came on brightly and then immediately disappeared. So I sat up in bed and looked at the clock and checked the time. After that I staid awake, knowing in my own mind that my father had died and that no one had notified me.

"About an hour and a half later my husband came into the door, and as soon as I looked in his face I knew what I had thought had happened had happened. He couldn't bring himself to tell me, so I told him that I knew that Daddy had died and that I knew the time. And the time that I told him to the minute was the time recorded on his death certificate at the hospital." (W1).

—*Dorothy Hand (Mrs. Jim) Wagoner.*

Grandmother Returns (WA)

A Gates County story tells of a mesage from a dying mother to her son soon after the Civil War, as told by Jimmy Moore of Hertford County.

My great-great-grandmother Priscilla Hayes Parker lived in the old Parker home at Sarem in Gates County. In her old age and widowed she delighted in keeping the homeplace alive with well attended flowers and shrubs. Here with her son Timothy she seems to have captured cherished memories of her livelier days.

Yet she had daughters in Norfolk whom she liked to go and visit. And upon one of these visits she was stricken with her mortal illness. She became possessed with a foreboding that she was going to die. That did not disturb her so much as the fear that she would never again see her home.

"We'll carry you home within a day or two," one of the daughters sought to console her while knowing that she was too sick to move.

Meanwhile Timothy, her son, was alone at the Gates County homeplace. One night he was sitting by the fire and thinking about his mother. He missed her and he felt miserably alone.

Suddenly Timothy's daydream was interrupted. There came a noise from upstairs. It sounded like someone walking. There came a call, "Tim, come up here, I've got something to tell you." It was his mother's voice. He got up, went into the hall and was at the foot of the stairway when he realized she wasn't there at all.

Next day Timothy received the news that his mother had died. She had died at the exact time the voice had called him. (M12).

—*Jimmy Moore.*

Buried Alive

Speaking in Wilmington, North Carolina, in 1890, Colonel James G. Burr told of how a deceased person communicated with a living friend.

Two young men of that city, he said, agreed that the first one who died would return and visit the other.

Not long afterwards one was killed by a fall from his horse, and a few days after the funeral the survivor was visited by the spirit of the deceased.

When buried the man was not dead as supposed, his spirit disclosed and then proffered, "Open the coffin and you will see I am not lying in the position in which you placed me."

The body was disinterred, and it was discovered to be lying on its face. (S11, IV, pp. 130f).

Ghost of Doctor Appears

Dr. J. E. West, drowned while attempting to ford Tucassegee River at Bear Ford on March 19, 1881, was said to have appeared two weeks later to the mother of one of his patients.

The apparition so impressed on her the necessity of recovering the doctor's remains that she dispatched a search party in accordance with the directions given. The corpse was found "in the precise place" she had pointed out. (C10, p. 280, n. 253).

21.
Guardians of the Living

The dead knows what the living is doing, but the living does not know what the dead is doing.

Now, in the latter part of the twentieth century, many of us feel that this belief may not be pure superstition. Yet many strange occurences give it some credit.

And there are some of us who go a bit further and say that the dead also has pover over the living. This most often is found where ties of family and friendship have been strong. In numerous stories a deceased mother or some other dear one returns in the spirit to comfort and care for the living.

A Mother Returns (BA)

There is little fear of such spirits, and a Southampton County, Virginia, black woman explains why. At twilight one day soon after the death of her mother this woman was sitting in her rocking chair when "my mama come and stand beside me."

"Weren't you afraid?" she was asked.

"Afraid! Afraid of my own mama, my own mama! My mama ain't going to hurt me."

"Well, why did she come back?"

"She want to see me. You know, she always want to know how I getting along."

A Gift of the Sacred Season (WA)

This motif is equally as popular in the white folk tradition.

Mrs. G. H. Pipkin of Murfreesboro, Hertford County, North Carolina, tells of the return about a century ago of her grandmother to look in on her small children.

Annie Futrell Sewell, the informant's mother, was but ten years old when her mother died in childbirth on a Christmas Eve bringing a sad Christmas season to the family and friends.

Santa Claus did not come to see the seven or eight Futrell children; instead, their father and friends distributed a few nuts and fruits among them.

Of course, there was the gift of the infant daughter; and when the child was ten days old, during the sacred season between Christmas and Old Christmas, ten-year-old Annie received a gift she would cherish the remainder of her long life.

This sacred gift came upon a quiet and sleepy wintry night. She and the other children had put themselves to bed; all but Annie drifted into slumber as the tall clock in the hallway ticked monotonously and bonged out the time when it had been customary for their parents to go to bed, at which their mother would come into their bedroom, tuck the covers snugly about them and plant a loving kiss on each one's cheek or forehead.

Annie had missed this loving care for many nights. But now there came to her ears the soft tread of footsteps. The bedroom door slowly opened, and a figure with fallen tresses moved from one child to another. It seemed to tuck in each child snugly and kiss it as her mother had done.

Annie, spellbound, looks into the face of her mother.

At last it came Annie's turn. Soft tender hands tucked the covers snugly about, and then there was a soft warm kiss. Annie opened her eyes and looked up; she radiated with happiness as she looked into the face of her mother.

The figure faded but the happiness continued. Although but ten Annie made certain that she would never be robbed of this gift from her mother. Next day she asked her father if anyone had visited her bedroom. He said no one had. (P10).

—Lollie Ruth Sewell (Mrs. G. H.) Pipkin.

Aunt Martha and the Orphan Girl (WA)

Aunt Martha Fleetwood, an aging black servant came to Hertford County with *Miss Vesta* when she got married. For Miss Vesta was the youngest of *Miss Caroline's* children, and Aunt Martha had attended her on the old Whichard plantation in Martin County.

Little is known of Aunt Martha other than that she was kind and devoted to the white family and that she seemed old enough to have spent thirty to forty years in slavery.

Miss Vesta died in 1898 at her new Hertford County home, the John Benthall place in St. Johns Township, when she gave birth to a daughter. This daughter grew up under the care of Aunt Martha to become the wife of Doctor R. Kelly White of Conway in Northampton County.

Mrs. White, thinking back upon her childhood, recalls that Aunt Martha had "a warm attachment for the Whichard family," from Miss Carolina, the grandmother, to the infant dranddaughter. She told the young motherless girl "things she thought would comfort me."

Often "I begged Aunt Martha to tell me about my mother, and she frequently did. She told me, for instance, she wanted me to kneel down beside my bed and say my prayers each night and that my mother would come and put her arms around me; and growing up with the belief that everything Aunt Martha said was true I felt my mother's arms around me . . . it was very real to me and a very comforting thing for a little child.

"And another one of the stories she told me was that each night my mother, Miss Vesta, as she called her, and Miss Caroline, as she called my grandmother, came and walked between the two chimneys on the upstairs roof of our house.

"That bothered me greatly, because I couldn't see that at night from my little bedroom, and I begged often to be allowed to go out and sleep in a cabin in the yard where Aunt Martha slept and where I thought I might be able to see my mother and grandmother. But I was never allowed to do it. One night I slipped out . . . but Aunt Martha knowing she would incur wrath if allowed it took me back very quickly.

"Incidentally, it was so important to me that I begged my father repeatedly. He told me (years afterwards) it would tear his heart out the way I would beg him to dig my mother's body up and let me see her.

"That is just one of the many stories that Aunt Martha told me. I loved her and she loved me. . . . I believed everything she told me at that age. As the years came I understood that she was telling what she wanted me to believe and perhaps what she believed, I do not know." (W9).

—*Mrs. R. Kelly White.*

The Return of Master Forbes (WA)

One century ago, Christmas Day 1873, Jessie F. Pugh's grandfather Forbes of lower Camden County, North Carolina, froze to death. He and others of a hunting party were caught on North River by a northeast ice storm. He was but twenty-three years old.

Forbes left his new wife Susan pregnant, and a son was born the following spring. Mother and child were attended by a devoted old colored woman, Aunt Emma, who had served the Forbes family from slavery days.

A few days after the birth of the child was the day of Forbes' return. Aunt Emma was moving busily about the house sweeping and dusting while mother and child slept in an upstairs bedroom.

There was a slight noise at the front door, not quite enough to announce a visitor but enough to attract the old woman's attention. Before she had time to wonder in came Forbes dressed in the same hunting habit that he wore that tragic Christmas day. Without acknowledging the presence of the old woman with a glance he walked lightly to the foot of the stairway, ascended the steps one by one, softly like the tipping of a cat, to the second floor where mother and son were sleeping.

Aunt Emma's hypnotized eyes followed his every move. He left the bedroom door open just like he wanted her to see in.

He paused at the bedside, and as Aunt Emma later told *Miss Susan*, "He des stan' dere, look at you, den look at de baby, look at you an' de baby . . . an' den he smile an' smile. I know he happy, caze he smile lak he smile when he wus a little baby."

With a heart full of happiness Forbes, the spectre,

'He des stan' dere, look at you, den look at de baby.'

moved silently from the room, down the stairs and out the front door.

"He at rest now, Miss Susan," Aunt Emma assured the mother after she had awakened from a peaceful sleep. (P18).

—*Jesse F. Pugh.*

The Woman in White (BA-J)

Until a few years ago a woman in white, a spectre lady, served as a kindly guardian of a Bertie County, North Carolina, tenant farm home.

Fourteen-year-old Jasper Porter of Murfreesboro says that this woman looked over him when he was a baby. At that time his mother Rose and her family lived there.

At night, after Rose had put her children to bed this lady, dressed in white much like a nurse, would come into the children's room and play with them.

As the little ones grew older Rose told them that quite often she would come into the room and find the ghostly lady standing over her children, looking lovingly at them and keeping them laughing. Each time that Rose came though the apparition would fade away.

Rose was not alarmed, for she took this to be the spirit of a kind woman. She had heard that about fifty years earlier a woman with a little baby lived in this house. One day a bad storm came up, and lightning struck the house and killed both mother and child. This woman's husband was so grieved that he moved away and was never heard of again by the people of the community. This woman, Rose supposed, was playing with her babies to ease her grief for the child she had lost.

After living here for a few years Rose and her family moved to Murfreesboro, but she kept in touch with her old friends in Bertie County.

Soon after she left the old place it came to be regarded as haunted, and it was ten years before the landlord was able to rent it to another family. And they wouldn't have it until he put in electric lights.

After all that trouble and expense, this family moved out quickly. The woman in white came back. But now she seemed very angry. She wore black clothes and scared the children and made them cry. Folks said that she must have been mad because she didn't like the electric lights.

The landlord burned the house down in 1972. Said he could find no one who would live there, and he wasn't going to keep on paying county property taxes on a place just for the ghosts to stay in. (B13).

—*Jasper Porter.*

The Little Girl's Ha'nt (WA)

Mrs. W. E. Kennedy of Norfolk, Virginia, was raised on the western borders of the Great Dismal Swamp in Nansemond County. Her family had many traditional stories, and her mother explained that an old colored mammy would entertain the white family with wonderful stories on many a cold or rainy day when the children were unable to go outdoors to play. She also did a good job of keeping them in line by telling them about dead folks who came back to *hant* folks still living, if they deemed it necessary. One of her favorites was about the plantation owner, *Marse Welson,*

Evangeline comes back to ha'nt almost every night.

who was very strict and pompeous. He ruled his slaves and his family as well, with an iron hand and everyone was afraid of him. His brother and sister-in-law died of *the fever* and left a little twelve year old daughter, Evangeline, who came to live with him. Evangeline was a very beautiful but spoiled and wilful little girl who liked to have her own way, and from the beginning she clashed with her uncle.

Their home was high on the banks and sloped down to the river's edge, and Evangeline loved to go down to the river to play. Her uncle forbid her to do it as it was steep, slippery and dangerous. She went anyway, every chance she got.

One day her uncle came upon her at the edge of the river and spoke so sharply to her it frightened her and she fell over the bank into the river. Marse Welson jumped in after her but the water was cold and swift and the tide carried her away and he couldn't find her. One of his slaves found her body about a mile down river next day.

Poor old Marse Welson was never the same again. Evangeline came back to *hant* him almost every night. Folks said he blamed himself for her death. After years of being haunted by Evangeline, Marse Welson lost his mind and died, blaming himself for her death. (K1).

—Mrs. W. E. Kennedy.

The Phantom Rabbit (BA)

Sometimes spirits of the deceased return as animals to help the living, as in a story from Hertford County, North Carolina.

Molly Gleason, a colored woman, would not let her son James visit his father's kin folks. They were not fit folks for his company, she contended.

But after awhile Molly died, and James had to go and stay with his father's kin folks. They made it hard for him, made him work hard and didn't give him much to eat.

Molly hadn't been in her grave long before she came back to help her son. He was in a back field plowing when a rabbit jumps into the furrow that he is in. He sees it is a rabbit thing, for it isn't scared of him at all.

Something told James that the rabbit was his mama, and that night when he went to the house from work he told his kin folks about it.

They say he is crazy and they are going to whip him if ever again he tells such a tale.

But next day the whole family was in the back field working, everybody chopping. And here comes that rabbit. She comes and jumps into the row with James, and she ain't scared of him at all.

His mama had taught him how to control *hants*. So he says, "What in the name of the Lord you want?"

The rabbit disappeared, just faded away. Everybody heard him and they saw it. They were so scared that they didn't treat James mean any more. (M10).

—*Dallas Moore.*

Grandma Comes Back (WA)

From down on *Lightwood Knot Road* near 'Possum Gut in Frenches Creek Township of Bladen County, North Carolina, comes a story of shape shifting. It was told to Dean Johnson of Rowan Creek community by one John Stringfield.

A group of young blacks were discussing hunting when one said he had bought himself a new shotgun and could hit any target he wished except one.

What was that? they all wanted to know.

Nothing but an old rabbit he had been wanting to get rid of. The family had been seeing the rabbit in the garden and closed up all the breaks in the fence they could find. Still somehow the rabbit got in.

"I shoot," he says, "the dirt fly up around her, and before I know it she's gone.

"You know, Grandma has been dead about four or five weeks; and Mama say that ain't no rabbit, that Grandma. She worried about all of us before she died, and now she is coming back to see how we are getting along." (J2).

—*Dean Johnson.*

Father Returns to Punish Son (BA)

With the family's interest at heart, sometimes the spirit of a deceased parent returns to discipline those who might be wayward.

This boy was mean even before his father died. He would drink and curse all the time.

After his father died he was meaner than ever. He treated his mother some kind of bad.

One day after sunset and after he had cursed out his mother he was coming by Old Lassiter Cemetery in Northampton County where his father was buried. It was getting dark, and something came out of the cemetery and beat him, beat him up bad, like with chains. He heard the chains just a-rattling, and he had chain marks on his body for a long time.

He knew that the Devil carries a chain like that, but he thinks it was his father, for he know he had treated him mama mean. (M10).

—*Dallas Moore.*

A Gentle Reminder (BA)

When a God fearing and hard working person dies the family must make certain that the example set be followed by each and every member as this Bladen County story illustrates.

A revival was set to commence at a Moore Swamp church upon a Sunday morning, and two sisters had agreed to clean the church building and brush the church grounds and the cemetery the Saturday before.

Come early that day Melissa was alone there on her knees scrubbing the floor while her sister Annie Mae was at home sleeping late. Annie Mae awakened but turned over on the other side. She was sleeping but knew she was just a-sinning.

Their mother had died a few months before, and she was buried there among the sandhill scrub oaks. The wind had scattered oak leaves everywhere.

While sleeping, said Annie Mae, she felt something like a hand pass over her, touching her lightly from head to foot. Her eyes were closed but she felt awake. Then a voice like that of her mother said, "Annie Mae, sin no more; sweep my grave white."

Annie Mae reported promptly for her task. And her sister remarked, "I know Mama see me down here scrubbing all by myself and you lying there in bed." (J12).

—*Nolon Johnson.*

The Accordian Player (BA)

The Reverend R. R. Lewis of Winton, Hertford County, North Carolina, says that his father, John Edward Lewis, had an accordian. He learned to play it well enough to play at dances.

But his mother didn't like his playing for dances. It was the Devil's work, she said. It was about 1908 and she was on her death bed when she called him to her side and made him promise to quit playing at dances.

But he went back on his word. About three weeks after her death he went to play for a dance and was returning home about three o'clock in the morning. When he came to a dark place in the path something like a white sheet jumped on his back, and it said, "I told you not to play for any more dances."

He never played for one again. (L7).

—*Reverend R. R. Lewis.*

The Drunkard (BA)

In a second story, this fellow was a heavy drinker. and his mother begged him to leave the bottle alone. But he kept right on.

After awhile his mother was taken gravely ill, but before she died she made him promise to quit drinking.

He promised just to humor her and to ease her worry, and after her death he went on drinking as bad as he ever did.

Then one night something come and slapped him off the bed, stomped him and railed, "You promised not to drink before I died. . . . You promise anything. . . . You better obey."

He obeyed, for that sobered him for the rest of his life. (L7).

—*Reverend R. R. Lewis.*

22.

The Dead Boss the Living

CERTAIN tales from antebellum times disclose that it was believed by the slaves that upon death a person's spirit might acquire uncanny powers over the living.

Thus the spirit of a deceased master or mistress was respected for supernatural attributes, and the onetime cringing slave in death acquired powers stronger than those of his master. One such story was related by a former slave woman of Northampton County, North Carolina.

Old Master Has His Way (BA)

"Old Master wuz right. He know'd dat nigger wuz no 'count all along," Betty Jane Futrell told her fascinated grandchildren, who would huddle about her spelled by her wonderful stories sometime near the dawning of the twentieth century.

The Civil War had thundered into memory about forty years past, but not before Betty Jane had served many a year as a house servant for the Walter Futrell family of eastern Northampton County near meandering Potecasi Creek.

Although she was a devoted and respected domestic she did not know the exact year she was born, but the white folks said it was about the time when *Old Nat Fray* (Turner) rampaged through Southampton County, Virginia, a few miles to the north, which was in 1831.

So she must have been climbing through her seventies with her long grey hair coiled and knotted and her strong featured face wrinkled with wisdom when the little ones loved to cuddle about her rocking chair and journey with her to her far away antebellum springtime.

Now, down the road apiece from Master Futrell's, said Betty Jane, lived one Zeb Vaughan, who had a large strong willed nigger called Zebo he used as overseer of his field hands. This Zebo was permitted to go here and there at will, almost like the white folks. And folks say he had a youngun or so on almost every plantation as far about as that old sorrel mule he rode might take him.

So one day he showed up on Master Futrell's plantation flashing a rabbit foot he carried in one pocket and a little sedge broom he carried in another. Back in those days some of the black folks jumped over the broom to get married, and folks about say that Zebo was always looking for a marriage for a night.

Zebo started hanging around the Futrell kitchen where Betty Jane was helping with the cooking, and Old Master Futrell got on to him when the silver started walking off with him.

About this time Zebo proposed, but Master Futrell was having no part of that no 'count nigger. He told Betty Jane he'd better not catch him hanging around his place any more. And when Master Futrell said that it simply was *that was that*.

Not long after that all the Futrell folks, whites and blacks, were crying and weeping; for Old Master took sick and died, and they placed him upon a gentle hill towards the woods where some of his young children already lay.

The women folks had barely taken off their mourning black before Zebo began hanging around the Futrell kitchen again and pestering Betty Jane. He pestered her right into saying that she'd marry him although she knew that Old Master would turn over in his grave at the very thought of it.

Zebo was in a hurry, but Betty Jane was strong willed. She wasn't going along with that jumping over the broom stuff, which wasn't even decent tor the field hands. She was going to be married like white folks or Zebo would have to go looking for a gal somewhere else.

The ceremony was set for one night. That would be easier on Zebo and all the field hands could be there too.

The folks gathered with the preacher in Betty Jane's cabin, a fair size comfortable structure near the great house. It had been a sunny day, but no sooner than dusk a white bone-chilling mist began to rise.

Then, as the preacher began, there came the roll of a far-off thunder in the east, an omen that may have disturbed some of the assembly. The thunder, rolling continuously, drew nearer and nearer, louder and louder until it passed the house and faded into the western distance.

The preacher paused and silence swept the room. Then with half-choked courage the preacher continued . . . only to be met with a louder thunder rolling from out of the east, mounting and then fading into the west.

The pause was longer, and the ceremony went forward with a quaking near whisper; and this was promptly silenced by an even louder rumbling along the former course.

Here come Old Master riding by.

This time the preacher's pause lasted and lasted, and nobody seemed to remember how long, while some of the folks slipped out and away. At last, he took up in a big haste. And he may as well defied the Devil without the Good Book in his hand. The thundering rose to the pitch of a boiling angry summer storm that sometimes swept over the Northampton cotton, tobacco and corn fields. It grew louder and louder as it seemed to follow the path leading from the eastern back field. Betty Jane's house began to shake, dishes fell off the shelves and crashed to the floor, and the house roof began to fall in. All the folks fled outdoors.

Then they saw. Here come Old Master riding by . . . in his old surrey all lighted up popping his whip over the heads of four white horses galloping like lightning.

Old Master vanished with all the thundering hoofs and thundering wheels. So did the folks, to other quarters.

Next day, sun shining bright, Betty Jane found her cabin standing sound, roof on, floors as clean as lye soap could make them, dishes on the shelves unbroken.

Zebo didn't put his foot on the Futrell plantation ever again. Betty Jane didn't see him at church, for he was such a big sinner.

Then Betty Jane, rocking climatically among her offspring, concluded, "Old Master wuz right; he alluz know'd the best. It wasn't long before I got me a good man, your grandpa. Now, look what good grandchillun I've got!" (M10)

—*Based on story by Dallas Moore.*

Ole Cesar Gets Best of Ole Dec Grey

In a story related by Mrs. Emily M. Baccus of Saluda, North Carolina, a mistreated slave man after death acquires supernatural powers over his evil master.

Aunt Patty's "ole man Cesar" belonged to "ole Dec Grey" whom she asserted "ware de deble." All the enjoyment Old Dec would permit Cesar was "when he get leave to come ober to stay a few days wid me an' de chillen."

One time Cesar got sick while visiting Aunt Pattie, and he died despite remedies administered by her and old mistress. Cesar knew his time had come, and he asked that he not be buried at Master Grey's place.

But Dec Grey sent mules and wagon and men after him. Now, there was a creek at the foot of the hill with water about two feet deep. Many a time these mules had splashed through the water like it was fun.

But this day "de water war plum low, an' de chillen an' I followin', an' de mules, dey step in de water brisk as you eber see, but Lord a-mighty! dat wagon jes' pull back on ole William. He cuss an' beat 'em to beat anythin', but dat wagon jes' pull back. Ole William say de deble in dat coffin, an' he go home hard as he can go, an' tell Dec Grey."

Old Dec promised to "whip de deble out ole William," and he came down to the creek to look on. They beat the mules "scandalous," but "dey couldn't pull ole Cesar ober dat water."

Now, Old Dec was "a mighty pious man" and there would be a lot of talk in church if he gave in to Cesar . . . "an' Cesar dade too." So he fetched six big hands to tote Cesar's coffin across the stream.

But Old Cesar was not to be outdone, and Aunt Pattie explained. "Dat ware four years come next

Monday week, an' blessed Jesus, ole Cesar done walkin' roun' old Dec Grey's same as when he ware alive . . . and when de ole Dec try to cross dat creek on hossback, no use, his hoss jes' stan' up on his hin' legs an' paw de air, an' he hab turn back, an' dey all say he can whip ole Cesar no more . . . "

And every Sunday after that Old Dec had to go a mile out of his way to get to church. Old Cesar won't let him cross that creek. (B1)

The Overlooking Mistress (WA)

Sometimes when a hard master or mistress died the spirit of the deceased made the slaves work harder than ever. Such a story comes from Lunenburg County, Virginia:

In antebellum times there was a Crow family who lived near Chase City in this county. This family had a large farm and worked many slaves.

The slaves were made to work hard, and this industry made the family exceedingly prosperous. This prosperity was reflected in many luxuries together with building of a large high house, the largest and finest for miles about. The height and massiveness of this structure caused it to be called *The High House*. It, too, was located on a hill, and one could view all parts of the plantation from it.

Eventually Mr. Crow died and left his wife Mary Ann a widow. Responsibility of running the plantation fell to her. The slaves soon learned that Mary Ann was a harder taskmaster than her late husband. Hot sultry days of summer she would sit at a window and overlook both her overseer and her slaves.

After many years, counted by the Negroes as years of eternal toil, Mary Ann, too, died.

The Crow slaves were disappointed that her passing did not lighten their work a whit. After her death passerbys reported seeing her still sitting by a window and the black folks at any time might see her from the fields . . . still overlooking.

By the opening of the twentieth century all of the old folks, white and black, had died. The old house had grown so haunted that no tenant would live in it. By World War I it had become so dilapidated that it was torn down.

Yet a beautiful, cool and clear water spring located where the dairy house once had stood still flowed on. It was called Mary Ann's Spring. To this day there are those who say that on dark nights one may see a light like that of a pitch pine torch travel from the old home site to the spring and back, then venture this is Mary Ann's Light . . . Mary Ann going to and from her dairy. (M1).

—*William I. Marable.*

The Old Man and the Junk (BA)

In one Negro folk tale an aging man who loses control over his family regains it after his death:

This old man had a lot of junk around his place, and he told his folks to take all of it to the blacksmith and make it up into hoes, shovels, plows and like that . . . something to work with.

But those folks were lazy; they didn't want anything to work with; and the old man had gotten so old they didn't pay him any mind like they did when he had his strength.

"You will do as I tell you one day," he warned them.

Soon after that the old man died, and the junk

hadn't been cleaned up and put to useful purpose.

One day the folks had come from working in the field, and they were resting up before retiring at night. All of a sudden something come through the hall dragging a heavy chain. Then they heard the old man's voice, "Didn't I tell you to get all this stuff up and carry it to the blacksmith shop before I died."

Them folks were badly frightened; couldn't sleep that night. Next morning early they gathered up the junk and carried it to the blacksmith to make up into working tools.

They weren't lazy any more. (B10).

Edward Beverly.

Didn't Like the Girl (BA)

Old Man James Kelly Woodley of Boykins, Virginia, was ninety-seven and had been seeing ghosts all of his life, because he had been born with a caul over his eyes.

"A lot of ghosts come back," the old man said, "come back to look after their kin folks."

Then he told of this fellow called *Big Pappy*. He had been dead four years and his son had grown up and started going out with this girl.

"Big Pappy didn't want that boy messing around with that girl. He knew that she was fooling around with other men and would get that boy in trouble.

"One night," said the old man, "when that boy go out with that girl, go for a ride, Big Pappy come and beat him up; you know his ghost beat him up and told him to leave that girl alone.

"And that boy did; he shore did! That boy married now; got a good wife." (W15).

—*James Kelly Woodley.*

23.

Ghost Magic and Controls

STRIKING a ghost portends dire misfortune, and even the sight of one may bring bad luck.

Among the Lumbee Indians, says Lew Barton of Pembroke, North Carolina, it is believed that a person struck physically by a spirit will surely die. He cited the story of one Amster Locklear.

One afternoon at twilight a figure approached Locklear as he sat on his porch, and it brought from behind "a hand which held something resembling a brush broom." It struck Locklear across the face. Angered, he shot the retreating figure with his shotgun.

About two months later Locklear was dead, shot in a brawl with his father-in-law. (B8).

Crooked Neck Queenie Gets a Man (WA)

In some folk tales the victim is not so unfortunate as in the Lumbee instance. But serious affliction usualy is the result, as in this Lnenburg County, Virginia, story:

"Some of them black gals who took their ducks to a po' market jes' couldn't see how *Crooked Neck Queenie* got herself the best man out of the whole neighborhood," declared Aunt Mary Ellis about 1910 while thinking back on her slavery days.

Aunt Mary had been the cook on Colonel Joe Ellis' plantation Eolian Hill near Chase City, Lunenburg County, Virginia. She was assisted by Queenie, a teen-age girl who was smart as a whip. Aunt Mary enjoyed Queenie's confidences, and she knew her story from its beginning.

Also on the Colonel's plantation was a young Negro called Mose. He made a pitch for Queenie, but she wouldn't listen to his sweet talk. She knew him for carrying a chip on his shoulder when things didn't suit him just right.

Now, this Mose went to the Colonel and says he wants to marry up with Queenie. But the Old Colonel wasn't raising niggers to carry down to Richmond for the Mississippi market. So he said it was up to Queenie; she could marry whom and when she liked.

At that Mose got that chip on his shoulder. Then he tells Queenie that every night he dreams that he is dead; and he says, "If I be dead, I goin' to fix you so ez no man'll want to look at you."

"Bless my old bones," said Aunt Mary, "if Mose's dreams of being dead didn't come true. The old Colonel had a big plantation and come cold weather there were a lot of rails to be mauled to keep up the fences about the fields.

One day Mose was with a group of several servants cutting heart pine trees from which to make rails. He ran as one tree was falling but caught his foot in a vine and fell beneath it. He was messed up so badly that folks got the cold shudders when they viewed his remains.

Winter days, winter months passed, but Queenie couldn't get Mose out of her mind. Even her daydreams were filled with his threat.

Spring came, and one twilight Aunt Mary had the kitchen door open while cooking waffles. She sent

Mose comes back and slaps Queenie on the neck.

Queenie with stacks of them for the Colonel and his family in the Great House. Returning she felt a presence and something slapped her on the neck. In the darkness stood Mose dressed all in white, except he had dropped his death mask and bared his ghastly face with its sunken eyes and protruding teeth.

Queenie was terrified. She fell into the kitchen door all doubled up. The Colonel sent for Doctor Bayne, but none of his ointments and salves would take the crook out of her neck. Aunt Mary sent word to Aunt Ellen, a herb woman also reputed for her skill at conjure, to come by for a social call. Aunt Ellen administered her herbs and uttered her incantations. But Queenie showed no improvement, and she apologized and explained that she had no power over the workings of the dead.

So Queenie's neck remained crooked as long as she lived.

But her life wasn't ruined after all. One thing that Mose hadn't counted on was Queenie's sweet disposition. There was a good looking young fellow on Old Hartwell Marable's plantation The Cedars two miles from the Ellis place. He came calling on Queenie and soon was head over heels in love with her.

They were married, and Queenie's husband was devoted to her as long as he lived, so devoted that there wasn't a one of several envious women of the neighborhood who could stir his interest a whit. (M1).

—*William I. Marable.*

Kicking the Dog Ha'nt

It is quite dangerous to molest an animal ha'nt as a story from Southampton County, Virginia, illustrates.

This man, he lived in Newsoms, Virginia, he was mean in his young days, but he wasn't so mean when I learnt him, but he was mean way back.

They say he met a old dog thing one time, one night. That thing running up toward him and he just turned around and kicked him. And so when he kicked him it slapped him, turn his head around, that thing turn his head around on his back.

He went to the doctor, but the doctor couldn't straighten it. I imagine he went to a conjure doctor after that, but I ain't hearn nothing of it. (B17).

—*Susie Brooks.*

The Spelled Car (BA)

Years ago Reverend R. R. Lewis was pastoring in Roanoke, Virginia, and he needed to go to Charleston, West Virginia, to attend to a business matter.

"Don't go," something seemed to warn him silently. But he pushed aside the warning and went on anyway.

About seventy-five miles on his way strange hindrances began to step in his way. His car lights went out. He had a mechanic check them; but the mechanic found no trouble and put the old bulbs back in.

A short distance from there, in a rough and hilly area, the lights went out again. This was away from everything, and he could summon no help.

But something told him, "Turn on your car light switch and go to sleep. Everything will be alright."

About three o'clock in the morning a rooster, which had perched on a nearby fence, crowed. "He woke me up, and I found my lights burning." (L17).

—*Reverend R. R. Lewis.*

The Spelled Gun (BA)

One night as I was returning home walking from town a dog thing came out of a big woods and followed along behind me, said one informant.

At first I didn't pay it much attention, but then it began to acting strange. First it would walk at my heels and then it would get close beside me. I would run it away, but always it would come back again.

I had my shotgun with me, and it aggravated me so much that I shot it from close up.

The thing didn't seem to be hurt; didn't holler and didn't fall over.

But my gun, that thing wouldn't shoot for two days. (F7).

—*Horace Futrell.*

Invoking the Trinity (WA)

In Perquimans County, North Carolina, an old man came back and put his daughter to a lot of trouble. She moved to first one place and then another trying to get rid of him. But somehow he found out where she was going and came along. He kept right on making those unbearable noises, the same old noises he made when he was living.

After awhile the old man began to get out of hand. One day she was gathering blackberries and was frightened by a bush snake. But when she spied a huge snake beneath a bush at her feet, Lordy sakes, that was too much. She couldn't put up with the old man's pranks any longer. And she thought what she could do.

So when she went back to the house and found him

making his same old noises, she called him over the coals. She spoke to him loudly, "What in the name of the Father, the Son and the Holy Ghost do you want?"

He couldn't stand that. He got away from there, and she didn't hear or see anything more of him. (B13).

—*Mrs. Lucius Blanchard.*

Laying the Ghost (WA)

This was a troublesome ghost. People had been hearing things at this old house, babies crying and women screaming. No one could live there.

So the owner called the witch doctor, and he went there to investigate and to lay the ghost.

He didn't have to wait long. Soon he heard knocking like someone shut up trying to get out. And this knocking moved from place to place around the house. So he put his hand against the wall and said in a loud voice, "In the name of the Father, the Son and the Holy Ghost what do you want?"

When this happened a tremendous force hit the wall where he was holding his hands, nearly knocking him down. Then a voice spoke out, "Help me!" and he said, "Lead me to you."

So the knocking, growing smaller, moved across the wall and stopped at a place near one corner. The voice spoke again saying, "Here."

So the witch doctor took the boards off the wall and found the skeleton of a baby which was thought to have been hidden by an unmarried mother.

He took the skeleton and buried it, ending the disturbances by the ghost. (C11).

—*Herbert Crouse.*

24.

Craving Ghosts

ONE must attend to all the wants of a dying person, otherwise one runs the risk of the person's ha'nt returning in queqst of fulfillment.

In both white and black tradition such ghosts may return to satisfy some craving, like companionship of a survivor, a thirst or hunger, desire for a cherished object, or to perform an unfinished task.

One informant succinctly put the black man's belief: "Unless you bury a person's things with him he will come back after them." (P17, p. 103). While ghosts of white people have a variety of cravings burial of personal objects is of little concern to them. Such beliefs are contained in the following stories:

The Phantom Coach (WA)

"John Alexander Rayner was my great-great-grandfather," says Jimmy Moore of Hertford County, in relating a strange incident which occured shortly after the Civil War. "He had two maiden sisters, Pat and Martha, who lived at the old Rayner homeplace in Bertie County between Powellsville and Cremo. A third sister, who had married the widower Lenow, lived in a small house down the road apiece."

Before the War Lenow had lived in Rocky Mount with his first wife. He was rich then, and now he delighted in telling the Rayners about his fine coach and many servants. Such stories were about the only riches both families had brought out of the war.

Having advanced in years, one Sunday afternoon Lenow became very sick and he was expected to die at any time.

Meanwhile Aunt Pat was sitting on the front porch of the Rayner home. Suddenly she sees this elegant coach coming down the road, a beautiful coach with a red capped coachman and two fashionably dressed black men standing behind, and drawn by fine black horses, stepping high. The coach carried only one passenger, a woman; it comes on down the road and goes around the corner towards where the Lenows lived.

Then, just about five minutes afterwards, word comes to the Rayner home that Lenow had just died.

Aunt Patty was much perturbed. She could find no other person who had seen the coach although she inquired up and down the road several miles.

Then she was convinced: Lenow's first wife whom he seemed to have loved so dearly was waiting for him. When he died "she came and got him." (M12).

—*Jimmy Moore.*

Old Man Wanting His Whiskey (BA)

"A *hant* will favor you, he will favor you if you give him what he wants; he shore will favor you!" said Alex Johnson, a logwoods worker who has held jobs in several southern states. He spent most of his boyhood with his parents near Marianna, Florida, and his grandfather in Halifax County, North Carolina.

"This old man, I forgets his name now, who pull the other end of the saw with me, he tell me.

"He say he know this old man who live alone and drink so much likker. He a hard drinker as long as he know him, but after awhile he stay drunk all the time. It begin to tell on him, it begin to tell when he drink anything he can get his hands on."

When folks told him that he had better ease up or *old red eye* would get the better of him he said, "I druther git my happiness here, for sure as hell I ain't going to get it down there."

So the old man kept right at it, drinking and drinking until he got down sick in bed. He couldn't cook and he couldn't get his whiskey. His folks would come over to his house and feed him, but they wouldn't give him a drop of whiskey.

He told them, " 'I'm going to die anyway!' " But his begging did no good. So the old man died calling for whiskey, calling for it like he was raving mad.

As soon as the old man was in his grave, his whiskey jugs thrown away and his house cleaned with lye some of his kin folks moved in and took over.

But they didn't stay in the old man's house the first night through. Along before bedtime the door fly open and here comes something like a turkey gobbler with a red cap on, and it tips through the house and

The old man comes back for his whiskey.

another door flies open and it tips on out.

"Bless you boy, them folks leave that house."

After awhile they found a family who would pay good rent. But in they moved and out they went.

"Bless you boy, things got after them."

Then they offered the old house for cheaper rent. After a long time a down-in-the-mouth family came along, and they were bad off enough to try anything. Next day they were asking for their money back.

"Bless you boy, they say them noises is too much for them."

After that the house staid vacant for a long time. When nobody would rent it those folks said anybody could have it rent free. They could stay there and keep it from rotting down.

"This here man tell his wife they is going to move in there and cut out that big rent they is paying.

" 'Are you crazy?' his wife scream.

" 'Mind now, mind me; I knows how to manage that old man.'

" 'How in de hell is you going to do that?'

" 'You knows I sells him whiskey when he alive. If he, his ha'nt, like his old self he be wanting whiskey now.' "

So the bootlegger argued his wife into the idea.

They moved in in about as big a hurry as the other folks moved out. First night they went to bed, and the old man didn't disturb them until after midnight. Then there come this terrible *blam,* which sounded like the back door had shut hard enough to knock itself to pieces.

" 'Git up and bar that door,' the woman tell her husband.

" 'The door, it's shut,' he say. 'I barred it on the inside before we go to bed. Now easy, don't get scared. The old man is already come, but he ain't going to bother you.'"

They didn't have to wait long before there came a roar, a terrible roar like a heavy wind wanting to twist the house roof off. But that man just kept his wife quiet. Then there came a tromping like horses' hoofs running around the house. Then the man went to the window and called his wife to come and look. They watched something like a big long dog with long fangy teeth hanging out of its mouth running around the house.

The man touched his wife's shoulder and whispered, " 'Git me that jug from under the bed.' " She slipped to the bed and slipped back, and she fetched the jug.

The man stuck the jug out the window and began to pour its contents onto the ground. His wife grabbed his arm and clamped down hard, " 'That's good whiskey!'

" 'I knows that!' and he nudges her off."

When the *dog* came around the house next it stopped beneath the window. There was the sound like a thirsty lapping. When the jug dripped dry the *dog* gave a long *slurp* and disappeared.

Then the bootlegger said to his wife, " 'I know all the time that it was Old Man Williams; he die dry and he is just wanting his likker. Now, he has got his fill and he won't be back.' "

And Old Man Williams never did come back, and the bootlegger and his wife saved a lot of rent money. (J1).

—*Alex Johnson.*

Old Man Tobe Wanting His Stick (BA)

Sue Mae's husband, Old Man Tobe Britt, lived to be over ninety years old. And for many years before his death he dragged himself around on an old walking stick. The stick went wherever he went, and no one saw him without it.

When he died they made the mistake of not burying the stick with Old Man Tobe. His daughter Emma soon found that out. He came back for it.

"I seed him one time," said Emma.

"He say, 'Seen my old stick?'"

"I say, 'No, I ain't seen your old stick!'"

"Then he go away . . . and I glad to see him go, for he got 'twixt me and the door." (S10).

—*J. F. Spencer.*

The Lady of the Rose Garden

This story was told in 1838 to Mary A. Hicks by Alfred Smith of Wake County:

Once I lived at a house where there was a rose garden located to the left of the front door steps. I used to sit on those steps and wash my feet after a hard day's work on the farm. One night, about dusk, I was sitting there when I saw a lady come up the path, and pause in the garden. I saw one white hand reaching out toward the roses, and then while I was looking down she disappeared; at least, when I looked up she was gone. For several evenings I saw her and it began to get on my nerves. Once day I mentioned the incident to a neighbor, who had been in that country for several years.

He told me a story of a young lady, who was always

frail, living there. Her lover died and after that she grew daily more delicate. Finally she died. Her last request was to have the cream rose bush planted on her grave. This was not done and so she was often seen in the garden, and always near the cream rose bush. I saw her often after that, but was never afraid, or nervous any more. In fact I considered her a friend and neighbor. (H6).

Old Man Wanting His Jacket (BA)

As a large boy, Jim Allen Vaughan, colored, was living in a log cabin at the John Porter place near the Hertford County, North Carolina, village of Menola. This house had a fireplace and a cat hole by which witches and ghosts might enter.

Henry Brown, a Quaker man, gave the boy a jacket which had belonged to one David Brown, recently deceased.

One night soon afterwards the boy prepared for bed as usual. He took care in stopping the cat hole and left the fire dying slowly in the fireplace. A lightwood knot, almost consumed in a bed of coals was going *poof . . . poof . . . poof . . .* as red flames threw flickers of pale light against the far walls.

During one of the flickers "I glimpsed at a shadow-like thing coming from the cat hole." Moments later, "I felt Old Man David's jacket come off my feet." With heart pounding, the boy lay frozen still. There he lay catching only fits of sleep throughout the night.

Come morning, "I found the jacket folded up and lying beside the fire logs. Then I was certain that Old Man David was wanting his jacket. I gave it back to Mr. Henry Brown but would never tell him why."

—*Jim Allen Vaughan.*

Aunt Betty Wanting to Cook (WA)

Many years ago, before it burned, there was an old house on a large Wake County plantation near present Wake Forest. Everything about it but one seemed ordinary. In antebellum times many slaves worked the fields, and colored servants did the cooking and served the meals. The white family was rich, idle and lazy.

As was customary, the kitchen—and this plantation had a large one—was separate from the *great house,* or the main dwelling, to which meals for the white family were brought and served. Separation of the buildings helped to reduce the fire hazard; and this was important, for once a fire got started in the frame structures a large bucket brigade of slaves couldn't fetch enough water from the well to put it out.

But a breezeway connected the kitchen with the dwelling. Cooking was done in a large fireplace in the kitchen basement, and a stairway led up to the breezeway and the dining room. This approach could be seen from windows and doors in several parts of the great house.

For many years during slavery Aunt Betty was the cook. She knew how each member of the white family wanted food prepared, and they would let no other servant cook for them. Aunt Betty cherished the compliment and jealously guarded her position. She got so that she would let no other servant in her kitchen except to assist with menial tasks.

But eventually old age grew on Aunt Betty; she became so weak and feeble that the cooking had to be done by another servant. Until her death Aunt Betty complained the job wasn't being done right. When they brought her broth she'd turn it away and say, "Let me git out of here an' hep me downstairs; dat woman doan even know how to make soup."

Then in time Aunt Betty's remains were buried in the family plot up on the hill, just outside the picket fence which enclosed the remains of Old Master and Old Mistress.

Soon, folks said, Aunt Betty was not resting in peace. On dark nights the white family or the servants might see a light move from the cemetery across the field to the kitchen. After repeated appearances it became known as *Aunt Betty's Light.*

After the Civil War time took a large leap from the past. The old plantation went down, tenants occupied the great house, and many of the family traditions were lost. But Aunt Betty wouldn't have any part of the new times.

A new family had moved in, and it was on a Sunday afternoon in the dead of winter. The mistress was preparing supper for her family and twilight shadows were coming early. She glanced at the open kitchen basement door and was startled to see the head of an old colored woman donned with a red bandanna. She fled into the great house. Moments later she returned with her husband, but the spectre no longer was to be seen.

Soon afterwards the woman was telling friends of the apparition. One woman said she was not surprised; she had heard of Aunt Betty; she explained, "They say that ever since Aunt Betty's death she has been wanting to cook in her old kitchen." But she has harmed no one.

Although assured there had been no kinder person than Aunt Betty the new mistress wished to have nothing to do with her. Shortly afterwards the family packed up and left the community, telling no one where they were going. (H1).

—*A. C. Hall, Jr.*

The Emphysema Patron (WA)

Virgilina is located in Granville County, North Carolina, and Halifax County, Virginia. Joe Glassock of this town tells of a strange occurence that took place many years ago at the old Danville Hotel.

One of the patrons had a bad case of emphysema. Each time he had a bad attack he would call the desk on his room phone. The clerk knew the meaning of his pitiful wheezing sound, and he would rush quickly to assist him.

After many years the afflicted man died. An attack was so severe that he could not get to the telephone.

But after his death his wheezing calls still came in to the desk. They were always the same choking calls for help.

Soon it got so that the management would not assign a guest to the emphysemic's old room. And to get rid of the ghost the room phone was yanked out and the old furniture removed and replaced with new.

That did no good whatever.

After awhile the calls quit coming. But this only after the old hotel was torn down. (H1).

—*A. C. Hall, Jr.*

25.

Scary Ghost Tales

'Come Up a Little Closer' (WA)

When Uncle Silas grew almost old enough for a call from Gabriel his master *put him out to grass* the same as he did the worn out mule that he had plowed.

He and Aunt Mandy, his old woman, were given use of their cabin and a garden plot in exchange for a few light chores.

Upon a summer day one might see the old man in his cane-bottom rocking chair in the shade of a sprawling wild mulberry tree, during a winter day in the warming sun in front of his cabin. Always a mongrel dog sprawled in complete laziness at his side.

The dog's name was Preacher, a name he earned in his younger years from the manner in which he talked to varmints he had chased up trees. Now, folks said, he too needed a walking stick.

Come darkness, Uncle Silas stood his walking stick in a corner of his cabin, slung an axe over his shoulder and walked forth in the night with the vigor of a young hunter while Preacher pranced and leaped about him expectantly.

'Possum hunting was all the pleasure this pair needed for complete contentment. And they delivered to Aunt Mandy 'possum after 'possum to fix up with sweet 'taters into a heavenly dish.

But Uncle Silas was taking his place in paradise too much for granted. Weather permitting, he hunted on Sunday nights. And Old Master warned him that could get him into trouble. But he had been getting by with it so long that he didn't worry a bit. So this Sunday night he went hunting as usual.

Old Preacher got on a cold trail, wandered here and there slowly and then got *hot*. He romped through a thicket to a grown up cemetery, treed yelping his head off.

Uncle Silas and his pitch pine torch came bobbing. Over the iron fence he went to the foot of a large holly tree. He waved his torch about to catch the varmint's shiny eyes before climbing up to shake him out into Preacher's jaws. No eyes shined, but Preacher said something was up there, so up the tree he climbed.

Up and up, he saw nothing, up until the tree top began to sway. Sadly he began to back down, when,

"Come up a little closes Uncle, come up where I can reach you."

Uncle Silas fell down limb by limb. Preacher tucked his tail between his legs. The pair hurried home in a flash, forsaking 'possum hunting forever. (H7).

—*Bob Hodgin.*

Plowing up the Cemetery (BA)

"There ain't enough money in the Rocky Mount banks to make me plow up another old cemetery," said Lawrence Diggers who has been working on Edgecombe County farms most of his life.

Diggers got his warning while he was living in the old house on the Cinders place between Rocky Mount and Tarboro. His boss man, who was living in Rock Mount, had rented the farm for its big tobacco allotment.

In the middle of the field was the Cinders family cemetery all grown up with shrubs and briers. One day when Lawrence was getting the land ready for tobacco transplanting the boss came out and said, "That old cemetery ain't doing no good; I want you to go over it with the tractor and the disk." So Lawrence did just like the boss said, and he plowed it up.

"I tell you Dallas, and I ain't telling you no lie," Lawrence asserted, "no boss ain't going to make me do nothing like that again.

"That night after I eats supper I goes out on the porch to pump a drink of water; and I looks out over the field and I sees a big bright light hanging over the old cemetery; it goes up and it comes down and it starts toward the house; and I runs and slams the door shut, I bars all the doors. We alls, me, my wife and the children, we alls go to bed. But I lays there all night, can't sleep, can't get to sleep.

"Next morning I goes out to the shed and starts the tractor, and I heads into the field. And I looks and I sees a white steam coming up from the old cemetery; ain't no wind, but it comes right at me like a dust cloud in March. It hits me hot, and it smells something like fried tainted meat. I runs the tractor back into the lot, and I goes to town and tells my boss to get another man; I ain't going to let my family stay on that place one more night." (M10).

—*Dallas Moore.*

Dennis Williams' Ghost (BA)

Dennis Williams died an old man about 1940. He had been born several years before the Civil War and in his old age he was the keeper of a small store in Northampton County's Occoneechee Neck. He played with children and delighted them with stories. June Green of the same community remembered one which told of the strange fate of Dennis' brother Johnny far back in the nineteenth century.

When Dennis and Johnny were young men they went traveling in strange country. They came upon a vacant house about nightfall and made themselves at home.

They built a fire in the fireplace and warmed themselves; but soon they heard a noise upstairs. They were surprised, for they had thought no one lived there. They asked who it was and were taken aback when something replied, "Ain't nobody but this poor old ha'nt!"

Still thinking it might be a prankster, they said, "Come on down." So the ha'nt did.

A human foot fell to the floor between the two brothers. As they backed away a second foot fell; then came a leg, another leg; then joint by joint and piece by piece all the parts of a human body fell and lay scattered about the floor. Then the parts set about knitting themselves together. When whole like a man the ghost put a spider over the fire in the fireplace and began cooking meat.

Johnny had been chewing tobacco and spitting juice into the fireplace; and the ghost warned, "You better not spit in my spider."

But Johnny, said Dennis, had a mean streak, and he couldn't stand for anyone to tell him not to do some-

All the parts of a human body fall to the floor.

thing. He'd surely have to do it. So Johnny spit into the ghost's spider.

The ghost flew into a rage. He snatched his spider from over the fire and began to whip Johnny with it. Dennis saw the ghost's eyes turn red, and he knew he had better get away from there. He ran from the house, ran as fast and as far as he could.

The last Dennis saw of Johnny was the ghost chasing him around the room. Next day he went back to where the house was. There was no house, no Johnny and no ghost. He never saw Johnny again. (G6).

—June Green.

Sleeping With the Dead (WA)

Doctor Godwin Cotton Moore, 1806-1880, who for many years practiced medicine at his home, Mulberry Grove, Hertford County, North Carolina, often told the story of a man who found a night's lodging in an humble home.

This man was passing through a strange country and was benighted. It was a desolate country with a few small houses spaced far apart. He stopped at one of these small houses and asked to be put up for the night.

The people were hospitable enough. They explained that they had only one room if he did not mind staying in that. That would do, he said; he had traveled far and was much in need of a night's sleep. So he was shown to a small dark room; and he immediately went to bed.

After some time he awakened, cold; he found that all the covers had been pulled off of him. Giving the matter little thought, he pulled up the covers and went back to sleep.

Again he awakened cold with all the covers off. Now, he thought the people of the house, although they seemed kindly, were trying to scare him. So he pulled up the covers; but instead of going to sleep he pretended to be sleeping while lying awake.

After a little while he felt the covers inching down, inching slowly toward the foot of the bed. He could see nothing there; it was too dark to see. So he carefully eased himself to a sitting position and then made a lunge for the foot of the bed. He grabbed a small body with his hands, the form of a child, a cold form that did not move. He lit a candle and saw that it was a dead child.

Next morning the family apologized. They had given him their only spare room. Their own child had died, and they had laid it out for burial across the foot of the bed to await burial. They thought their guest would not discover the corpse in the ill-lighted room. (C5).

—Mrs. Margaret Colvin.

The Squeezing Ha'nt (BA)

"Me and my boy friend were out walking near Hobgood in Halifax County. We had come down a hill through a cemetery.

"When in the cemetery something grabbed me from behind. I couldn't get loose. I cried for help, and my boy friend pulled me.

"When I got loose I was plumb out of breath. A ghost takes your breath away." (J11).

—Mary Johnson.

Lulu Frightens the Mule (BA)

"Yessir, I shore does, I believes that a mule or a horse can see ghosts," said Carey Pridgen of Bladen County's Moore Swamp community on Black River. "And it ain't been more than five or six years when my brother Hardy was driving that big old black mule with a cart full of folks up there above Jessie Murphy's. It was along about night when they go between the graveyard and the Big Bay.

"All at once the mule stops, he acts like he is seeing something, and Hardy sits there wondering.

"Hardy say he don't know why he did it, unless it was to scare them women folks with him. He say, 'Look out there Lulu, don't you do that!' And that mule turned around and she almost throw'd them out of that cart. And she come back.

"Lulu been dead about two years, you know. She was getting old, and she told a lot of ghost tales before she went away.

"Yessir, I believes that was Lulu up to some of her devilment, and that mule saw her." (P16).

—*Carey Pridgen.*

The Werewolf of Pasquotank (WA)

A man who lived at Weeksville in Pasquotank County, North Carolina, had a large dog. Neither the man nor his dog were very good neighbors. The man was a heavy drinker and the dog was large and mean.

The dog bit a neighbor, and his master agreed to get rid of him. He was so attached to the dog that he did not want to kill him; so he carried the dog to the south side of the Albemarle Sound and gave him to a family.

Not long afterwards the man went on a long drunk. He drank so heavily that his whiskey gave out, and he drank wood alcohol and died.

Three days after the man's death, after his body had been buried, his aunt and several other people were greatly alarmed to see a strange looking creature approach the houses from the woods. The thing seemed to be a cross between the dog and his master, had a dog's body and a man's head.

In the aftenoon when the aunt was hanging out clothes the horrid thing trotted by the woodpile near the clothes line. She looked and screamed, "Oh my Lord!" Then she ran into the house. When she looked out through a window the thing was gone. She wondered if it was because she called the name of the Lord. (H1).

—*A. C. Hall, Jr.*

Tastes Dead Woman's Piclkes (BA)

When one of Lonie Mae's neighbors died she went over to her house to help tidy up things. While in the kitchen she removed a jar of the dead woman's pickles from the shelf, and she took a taste of them and put the jar back in its place.

That night when Lonie Mae laid down to go to sleep the sheet began to slip off of her. She got up and fixed the covers, but the sheet slipped off of her a second time.

The second time was enough. "I began to wonder if that woman didn't object to my fooling with her pickles," she confessed, "so I went into my son's room and lay down on his bed." (M10).

—*Dallas Moore.*

26.

The Treasure Guardians

Stories of hidden treasure and their guardian spirits were numerous and very popular throughout the nineteenth century. Virtually every community had its haunted house and restless ha'nt of some deceased person who had not disclosed the hiding place of his or her money before death.

Travelers carried along a bag of such tales for the amusement of families which might accomodate them overnight.

Along the coast and upon tidewater rivers pirates hid chest after chest of silver and gold and gems.

There was a practical interest in hidden treasure. All too often colonial and state currencies were so unstable that people lost confidence in them. Gold and silver coins were a more reliable media of exchange, and they commonly were used as savings. Without banking facilities, the people often kept their savings on their persons or on their premises. So hidden treasures have been found, but their value was but a fraction of that represented in folk tales.

Treasure ghosts came in different types. There were those of gentle people who wished nothing more than to bestow their riches on some deserving person. Others were evil and vicious, determened to hold onto their riches after death. If an evil person, like a pirate, had entered into a pact with the Devil, it was all but impossible for a human to recover the treasure.

In the Celtic countries it was believed that a person's affairs must be properly settled for his spirit to rest in peace.

In one instance, a poor but honest Scotchman had borrowed some farm tools from a neighbor and a sudden death prevented him from returning them. Whereupon his ghost haunted another neighbor until those things had been returned.

It took some violent doings before the neighbor was convinced he must take action. He demanded of the ghost what was his business, but unfortunately the ghost's jaws first had to be unlocked. To do this the man had to seize the ghost "as he would a bush of thorns" and lift his feet off the earth that air might pass under them. Upon which the ghost's unlocked jaws "began to speak in so sepulchral a tone as to palsy all who heard it."

Return of the tools accomplished, all hauntings ceased. (S14, pp. 39-44).

Among both white and black Americans the common way to get out of the power of an evil caliban is to address him in the name of God and the Trinity. One might say, "What in the name of the Lord do you want?" (P17, p. 140). The ghost is either supposed to go away or lead one to the treasure. In Hertfordshire one would say, "In the name of God, who art thou?" (L4, p. 33).

One colored man had a sure-fire way to get rid of a ha'nt: "If a ha'nt bodder you, ax him for some money an' he'll sho' leab." One old man, caught in a haunted woods one night, started taking up collection and the ha'nts fled. (P17, p. 141).

In Beaufort County, North Carolina, one finds the belief that "a century will do away with a ghost" provided the proper requirements have been fulfilled. (F5).

But this does not seem to hold with all pirate treasure ghosts which haunt North Carolina tidewater from Knotts Island on the Virginia line to Southport on the Cape Fear River.

At Bath in Beaufort County it was discovered in 1918 that a phantom treasure hiding party returns every one hundred years to reenact the original burial and to renew the magic of the guardian spirit. (W6).

Treasure tales are so numerous that only a selection may be offered.

The Anderson's Mill Treasure (BA)

This tale by Jim Shaw, a Hoke County, North Carolina, native, is from a tape recording:

I heard my grandaddy tell about a treasure in a old field at Old Anderson's Mill. A place up in the field wuz ha'nted. And I believe there was something up there.

And one of the girls wuz picking cotton, and she see fifty cents on the ground. She grabbed at it and she missed it and it disappeared away.

Joe Morrison, the man what dig money, he told 'em there wuz some money there, and he went and marked the place, and a whole bunch of them went there whut dug money, you know since the Yankees come through, and stuck up a stob there where he thought the money was, and he wait until a certain day of the moon and go there and dig it that night.

And he went back there to steal it; he thought he could do it; he had a *wagging rod*, one of them little *wagging rods;* and he bumped down in the ground; and he went back to steal it.

And he got to digging, sprinkled something all around on the ground so a ha'nt couldn't get in there, and said he got down there and dug and dug; and

He went off crawling frightened half to death.

stuff begin to looking green, and he looked over there to see what the matter and there was a great big bull scrounging him up in the hole pushing him out of there. He went running and he never did go back.

And say another man went down there next night. He was just as nervous, and he stuck his rod down there, and he went to digging. He said he heard a rumbling in the air, and he was a colored fellow, and say all at once a white woman come right down there and stood with a parasol over her head. She looked him right in the face and said, "What in the world are you doing?"

Say he went crawling off half frightened to death hollernig, "Nothing . . . nothing . . . nothing."

And they never did get that money. (S4).

—*Jim Shaw.*

The Golden Wheels (WA)

Years before the Civil War a man by name of Condrey came to North Carolina's Pungo-Pamlico area. He was quite industrious and made a large amount of money. Local people said that he never spent it. Instead, he buried it near his home on Wright's Creek.

Condrey died without telling anyone where he had hidden his money. Years later one Sam Wilkins, a poor fisherman, invited Junius Fulford, a fellow fisherman, to help him look for it. Sam explained that he had been having visions, and "I see gold wheels going over and over when I go past that place."

Junius wanted no part of Sam's digging, and he supposed that Sam went at it alone. It certainly seemed so a little afterwards. He stopped talking about gold wheels and began spending old coins at the local store.

After that no strange apparitions have been seen at the once ha'nted place. (F5)

—*A. Dean Fulford.*

Pirate Treasure Hunters (WA)

Many years ago Aunt Delphia Stowe O'Neal lived on South Creek near the village of Aurora. As a traditionalist she was one of several people of this community south of the Pamlico River who told pirate treasure stories.

Aunt Delphia's son Frank and a neighbor, Clarence Freeman, dreaming of fabulous riches, undertook to accomplish what the legenday treasure seekers always had failed to do.

With the help of Aunt Delphia's advice and a *money rod* they located a site upon the Pamlico across from Bath. One night, with their lantern, they followed a path to it through inky darkness.

Carefully, they followed all the procedures laid down by Aunt Delphia. As silent as the darkness itself they sank their hole, and their hopes swelled as "they got up on the money."

But when a spade hit a solid object "there came a booming like the mauling of a hollow tree. A fiery red light rolled into the hole with them, and from just above their heads came a thunderous roar like the wings of partridges."

Unnerved by the blinding light and the tormenting sounds the treasure seekers dropped their spades and ran. Days later they summoned enough courage to return to their digging site. It was not to be found; a scrub thicket stood where they thought it was.

Frank and Clarence gave up treasure seeking and contented themselves with adding their story to their community's treasure of folklore. (F5, F6).

—*A. Dean and Mrs. Junius Fulford.*

The Lights of Raby Woods (WA)

A hundred or two years ago *Pine Tree* was an obscure settlement in Hertford County, North Carolina, between Powellsville and Bethlehem, and about a mile more to the northeast on the way to Pitch Landing on Chinquapin Creek was *Raby Woods*, large, dark and ha'nted.

Some time before the Civil War, according to legend, the Raby family lived in this area. The elder Raby prospered from his plantation and pitch and tar production.

But Raby's son was not as industrious as his father. Like too many young men of the gentry he preferred to idle and squander. In this way he got into the clutches of some card sharks. He ran to his father for help, but his father cut him off instead. He was going to teach him a lesson.

To protect his savings against theft the elder Raby packed his money in a keg and set out to hide it in the great woods.

But the son followed his old man, and when he had gone he proceeded to help himself. But the father returned to make certain his treasure was safe and discovered the theft. Father and son got into a big fight, and they killed each other.

Thereafter people called the woods of the big fight Raby Woods, and they found that it was haunted.

Some hunters began to avoid the place. They could hunt around it at night and see nothing unusual. But the minute they entered the woods their dogs would begin to act strange, whining like they were afraid. At that the hunters might look up and see two lights moving around the tops of the trees and acting like angry people. They would run for each other and swallow each other up, then part and do it all over again.

"It's Old Man Raby and his son," they say. "They are still fighting over that money which still hasn't been found after these two hundred years." (M9).

—*Jimmy Moore.*

Drives off Worthless Husband (BA)

This man kicked his wife out of their home and she had no place to stay. She walked through the country hoping to find some work.

When night came she stopped at an old abandoned house and made a fire in the fireplace to warm herself.

As she was about to look for a place to lie down for the night she heard something coming down stairs. She looked and saw that it was a man without a head with a knife in his hand. She was badly frightened.

As she stood shaking the ghost asked, "What in the name of the Lord are you back here wandering?"

At that time a head came on the thing; and it told the woman that long before it had buried a treasure and she could have it and the house too.

The thing led her from the house to the hiding place on an old farm and she dug it up.

The woman fixed up the house; her husband found out that she was rich and he came to stay with her.

The first night he was there the headless man came down the stairs with his knife and chased him away.

The ha'nt told the woman, "I don't want that worthless man spending any of my money."

The husband went crazy and soon died. The woman got a new and industrious husband; and the thing let him alone. (B10).

—*Edward Beverly.*

The Devil's Treasure (BA)

It is virtually impossible for a person to recover a treasure that is guarded by the Devil, as this black folk tale demonstrates:

One day a white man loaded his treasure on an old wagon and had this colored man go down in the woods with him.

The white man said to the colored man, "Will you take care of my money?"

Thinking he might have it to spend, the colored man said, "Yes, I will look after it for you."

But the white man cut the colored man's head off and buried his head beneath and his body above the money. Then the white man died without digging up the money.

Now, all had sinned . . . the white man and the colored man . . . and the Devil got into that money and he would let no one dig it up.

One time some men started digging and something "like a big bull come running, come scare them away."

Another time more diggers came, but "the Devil turns like a rattlesnake and begins striking at the diggers."

When a third group of diggers came the Devil appeared "like a man with two big feets . . . one red eye."

And again he "makes like a train coming through there . . . the woods . . . sounded like it was going to run right over them."

After all that, some diggers got a preacher to read the Bible over the treasure to cross up the Devil. But that was an evil thing to do, and the Bible fell out of the preacher's hands . . . "and nobody never did get the Devil's money." (J1).

—*Alex Johnson.*

Cutting out the Landlord (BA)

This man and woman were traveling one time. They were looking for a place to spend the night, and they came to this old house that no one lived in.

The woman had a little baby, and the man decided to go and ask the owner of the house, who lived a mile away, if they could stay there that night. So he left the woman and the baby there.

The landlord said, "You can stay there if you want to, but nobody has been able to stay in that house. The ha'nt always runs them away."

The man was frightened, and he said, "I ain't going back there."

The woman got tired of waiting for the man to return, and she went in the old house and laid down. Then after midnight, between twelve and one o'clock, she heard noises. The house had a stairway, and the house lit up. Something came down with no head. The woman was scared to death.

The thing asked, "What do you want?"

The woman had heard that a ha'nt could be controlled by calling in the name of the Lord, so she said, "In the name of the Lord don't hurt me." She then told the thing that her husband had gone away and had not returned.

"I ain't going to hurt you," the ha'nt said. There is some money around here I've been wanting to give to somebody." He then told her that it was "under that old chimney."

Next morning, after it had got light, the husband returned to the old house where he had left his wife. He was surprised to find her alive. They dug under

—*Wash Vaughan.*

the old chimney, found the pot of money. They kept it, because the ha'nt didn't want the landlord to have any. (V7)

The Miser's Money (BA)

This story was heard in Brunswick County, Virginia.

There was an old man who lived alone and wouldn't spend any of his money. Year after year, his neighbors said, he got richer and richer. Then he died without telling anybody where he was keeping all that money.

People dug all over the place, dug up all the apple trees and peach trees and pear trees, and they found no money. They tore up the hearth and looked all over and under the house, and still they found no money. But they knew money was there because it was so haunted that nobody could stay there. But there was a man and his wife who said they would give it a try. They moved in.

One day when the woman was in the house alone this thing came and ran through the house with a big *clomp, clomp, clomp*, and jumped into the middle of the bed.

The next day it came and did the same thing; and every day it came and jumped into the middle of the bed.

The woman saw that it was trying to tell her something. So she got her scissors and cut the bed mattress open. Inside with the shucks she found a fortune . . . twenty thousand dollars.

The old man's ha'nt didn't come back any more. (D6).

—Littleton Dromgoole.

27.

Laughing With the Ghosts

'Marster Cornelius Let Me Go' (WA)

In his old age Uncle Roger was a frequent visitor to the bar on the main street of the Northampton County, North Carolina, town of Jackson. As the nineteenth century was closing this was the favorite collecting place for certain of the gents of the town.

Uncle Roger was always welcome. He had served the late Doctor Cornelius Moore as coachman most of the doctor's long term of practice.

The affable hat-tipping, low-bending, white haired colored man was humored by the white guests, particularly those who had been close friends of the old doctor, always with enough whiskey to warm his insides, ease his rheumatism and loosen his tongue. Whereupon he would entertain the house with one fabulous tale after another from the old times.

One night a playful white man got Uncle Roger a bit too drunk. When the subject of ha'nts somehow got in the conversation he boldly professed that he was never bothered with such, even those of the more vicious sort.

Upon this the white fellow challenged, "Uncle, I dare say you will not go and touch the iron fence around the grave of your old master." Doctor Cornelius Moore had been buried in the Episcopal Churchyard on a nearby street.

"You knows like I does that I ain't afeard of my old marster," the old man asserted taking slight offense.

Immedately the playful white man wanted proof.

Then as Uncle Roger stumbled off towards the cemetery the white man took a short cut and hid in a clump of shrubs beside the grave.

After a brief wait Uncle Roger came staggering up. He wove his way though the iron gate and steadied himself against his old master's headstone. Whereupon the white man reached up, grabbed him with an iron grip and held him tightly against the stone.

Uncle Roger's whiskey stupor quickly cleared. He hollered, "Marster, Marster Cornelius, let me go, Marster, let me go!" After a few moments the old man couldn't be held. He broke loose and raced for the brightness of the Main Street gas lights. He was still crying, "Marster, Marster Cornelius, let me go!" as he broke into the barroom. The gents soon discovered that he had gone raving mad. And a few days afterwards he was taken to the insane asylum.

They say he died soon after that, he died crying for his old master Cornelius to let him go.

They buried the devoted old servant in a plot near to his old master.

Some folks say they made a big mistake.

They insist:

Take almost any dark and rainy night now, way after midnight and way before cockcrow, one may go by Doctor Cornelius Moore's resting place in the Episcopal Church burying ground and find that the old doctor may be resting in peace but the spirit of his devoted old servant is not. There beside the doctor's tomb something is holding him by the tail of his frock coat in which he was buried, and he is crying,

"Marster, Marster Cornelius, let me go; Marster, Marster, let me go!"

—Jimmy Moore

'I've Been Coming Back' (WA)

For a long time no one would dare to spend the night in this old haunted house. At last a foolhardy black man was induced by a wager to undertake a night there.

Soon after the light was out and the man was in bed he looked and upon the foot of his bed sat a big black cat with eyes like moons licking his wiskers. Then the cat mewed, "There ain't nobody here but you and me, is there?" The man rose up and said, "Naw, there ain't gwine to be nobody here but you long." And with that he went out the window, taking the window-sash with him; and down the road he bolted like a streak of lightning.

Out of breath, the man sat down on a log beside the road to rest. Looking up there was the same black cat sitting on the other end of the log. And the cat mewed, "That was a right good race we had." With that the fellow said, "Dat ain't nothin' to what we's gwine to have."

Next morning those who had made the wager went looking for the black man; only the smashed window sash suggested the turn of events the night before.

The full story was disclosed two or three days afterwards when the man came straggling in all bedraggled and with clothes half torn off. When asked where he had been all the time he answered, "I've been coming back." (C10, p. 325).

Riding the Ha'nt (WA)

Years ago and a few miles southwest of Rich Square, Northampton County, North Carolina, a small country church sat upon a knoll of high ground. A long span of steps led upward from the grounds to its front door.

Arrangements had been made for funeralizing a black brother, but a late afternoon storm that lasted into the night brought postponement of the concluding services. However, the corpse was left in front of the pulpit.

Meanwhile a country fellow was trying to make his way home between showers, stopping at first one shelter and then another. But the storm was so persistent that he was overtaken by night, and a heavy rain drove him into the church.

This fellow, unnerved by the fierceness of the storm, walked down the aisle almost to the pulpit to be as far from the thunder bolts as possible.

The electrical display was spectacular. Lightning flashes illuminated the church, and this fellow caught a glimpse of the deceased brother lying in his open casket. He was so frightened that he ran from the church into the storm, falling down the long steps on his way. He fell on the back of a billy goat which also had sought shelter. The goat took him away on his back, and as the lightning flashed he saw that he was astride some hell bent white creature.

The bumpkin fell off and ran two miles home through a downpour of rain. He fell speechless in his doorway, and it was some time before his wife's first aid enabled him to give words to his frantically moving lips. (S7).

—*Claude Smith.*

No Trouble at All (WA)

Years ago Joe and John, aliases for two characters, went visiting together one night. And in those days Gates County, North Carolina, produced large orchards of apples, and their host had an abundance of apple brandy.

They passed a very pleasant evening drinking, swapping yearns and gaming. Late into the night Joe decided it was time to go home, but John wanted to stay on awhile longer.

Joe set forth alone. After a short piece he left the main road for a *short cut*. The path was too narrow for him, and he staggered off into a cemetery. There had been a death in the neighborhood, and grave diggers had dug the grave. And Joe staggered right into the grave. He scratched around trying to get out, but he was too drunk. He slumped into a corner and fell asleep.

Later on John decided it was time to go home. He took the same short cut and he also staggered off the path and fell into the open grave. He started scratching and woke up Old Joe.

"You ain't going to get out of here," said Old Joe.

At that Old John came out of there without any trouble. (F1).

—*Billy Felton.*

Preacher Wants the Same Chance (WA)

In a Halifax, North Carolina, story:

This preacher was in the midst of a hell fire and damnation sermon and had his audience completely mesmerized. The flames of hell were cracking and his listeners were poised like rabbits ready to jump when he paused and then asked,

"Will you be ready when Gabriel blows his horn? Will you be ready to run a race with the Devil? Will you be ready . . . ?"

Before opening of services a boy with a horn had hidden in the church loft, and he gave his horn a toot.

There was complete silence as the congregation sought to learn the source of the horn blast. Then the preacher put the question a second time, "Will you be ready when Gabriel blows his horn?"

The boy blew long and loud. The entire assembly aimed for the door and streamed from the church. The preacher followed, but on his way out his frock coat got caught in the swinging double door and he was stopped on the door steps. Whereupon he pleaded, "Turn me loose, Gabriel; please turn me loose; give me the same chance as the others." (J3).

—*Jack Vaughan.*

How to Get Home (BA)

Two black men were out together one night. Each one thought that he was following the other and both got lost.

Soon one asked his companion, "Do you know how to get home?"

"No," came the reply. "Do you?"

"No," said the first one.

They walked on apiece and this little old man . . . a ghost . . . got after them.

Then one asked the other, "Do you know how to get home now?"

"Yes!" came the reply. "Run! run! run like hell!" (B10).

—*Edward Beverly.*

'I'll Knock Your Head Off' (BA)

A good many children of rural North Carolina are being told ghost stories by their parents, grandparents and other relatives. We'll take a *tar-baby* like one from Maney's Neck Township, Hertford County.

This father and his two brothers went out walking one cloudy night. But there were some openings in the clouds which sometimes let the moonlight through.

They came to this big old house that no one had been living in for many years. Thickets of shrubs and tangles of vines had grown up all about it. They were surprised to see a man-looking thing standing beside the road in front of it.

The father and his brothers spoke to it, but the thing didn't reply, it didn't say a thing. Instead, it looked straight at them like it is looking right on through them.

The father's temper began to rise: "You better speak to me or you'll be sorry." But the man-thing just grunted "m-m-m-m . . ."

The father was a right strong fellow and he knew it. Wasn't no man around he couldn't whip. So he said, "Better speak to me or I'll knock your head off." But the man-thing just says, "m-m-m-m . . ."

The father waited to give him time to answer, and then he slaps him hard. And the thing's head does really fall off.

The two brothers ran away; and the man-thing picked up his head and ran. He loped down the path like a scared dog. (W12).

—*Tony Wiggins.*

The Grave Robbers (WA)

There was this rich woman who died, and her jewelry was buried with her. A night or two afterwards two boys of the neighborhood came to steal the valuables from the grave.

This was when people told ghost stories, and this particular graveyard was supposed to be haunted.

The boys were afraid, and they felt uneasy as they made their way through the dark night toward it.

A grey and ghostly fog, which had spread over the ground hiding the path, added to their anxiety. They bumped into each other and other things.

"Don't you suppose we should wait for another time?" one asked.

"It'll be alright when we get into the field, into the open," the second one assured.

They found the grave, dug it open and removed all the jewelry, all but one piece. This was a ring which was too tight on a finger to slip it off. They wanted everything, so one took his knife and cut off the finger.

The woman was not dead; she had been in a coma instead. She awakened and sat up in her coffin. She began to thank the robbers for saving her life. This so completely unnerved them that they ran away terror stricken. The more she called the faster they fled. (Val).

—Horace Vaughan,

28.

There Ain't No Ghosts

'I'll Fix You' (WA)

Jake Peele was an imaginative and fascinating story teller, particularly when he went to the general store at Winsteadville, Beaufort County, North Carolina, on a Saturday night and the storekeeper primed his tongue with a drink of whiskey.

One Saturday night, not long after the death of one Robbie Smith, Jake told of his encounter with Robbie's ghost.

A few nights earlier, Jake asserted in a matter of fact manner, he butted into Mr. Robbie as he was passing his house with his mule and cart. He suspected that he had ghostly company when a trace chain, one of a new set, came loose. Jake got down and fixed it, hooking it securely. A short distance further on the trace chain on the opposite side came off. Jake fixed that one securely too. Nonetheless, the two trace chains began coming loose one after another. When this grew troublesome he said, "Now, Mr. Robbie, time you stopped aggravating me."

Soon Jake knew Mr. Robbie was paying no heed to his suggestion; the chains broke loose again and again. By now about all of his patience was gone, and he raised his voice and said harshly, "Mr. Robbie, I going to fix this here chain one more time, then I'll fix you. I'm going to leave this old mule and cart *with you*, and I'm going to walk on home."

Mr. Robbie took the hint. Said Jake, "What in the hell could he do with my old mule?" (A1).
—*Mrs. Minnie Hollowell Allen.*

Uncle Jake's Ghost (WA)

Old Uncle Jake lived alone for many years in a small house near Savages Station in Gates County's Hazlett Township. And in his old age he grew eccentric. And after his death his ghost—so they say—took up where he left off.

Several families attempted to live in his old house, but his ghost didn't want them around. All left after brief stays. It got to where no one would dare to move into the old house.

After awhile a neighbor bought Uncle Jake's place, and since there was no chance of getting rent money he decided to store peanuts in the house.

One day the new owner was at a community store when his two colored helpers came running, half out of breath and swinging their heads, "Boss, Uncle Jake won't let us store no peanuts in his house!"

The boss learned that his hired hands had heard a thumping noise overhead after they had tossed a couple of bags of peanuts into a downstairs room.

Wanting no delay in the work, he told them, "Come on with me; I'll go with you to Uncle Jake's house and show you there's nothing to be afraid of."

The storekeeper overheard the conversation, and he saw how he might have som fun. He closed his store, cut across a field and arrived at the haunted house ahead of the white boss and his two colored helpers. He hid upstairs.

The white landlord walked boldly into the house, stomped on the floor, glanced about and bellowed, "Well! Uncle Jake, how are you today?"

"Only tolerable . . . tolerable," replied Uncle Jake through the storekeeper.

White boss froze. His hired hands gazed at him. After a moment he ran from Uncle Jake's house with his helpers close behind. They sped to the pickup truck waiting beside the public road.

No peanuts were stored in Uncle Jake's house; and Uncle Jake's ghost got complete possession of it until the elements tumbled it down. (B14).

—*Sam Boone.*

There Ain't No Ghosts (BA)

Some people say, "What is ghoses?"

This man say, "I grown man and I ain't never seen no ghoses? Why you all seen it and I ain't never seen it?"

But time come, he say one night he go off and is coming back, say he pass this old house where a man lived before he got killed, and along about two feet from the house he hear a horse coming . . . running, running, running. He looks up and he don't see no horse head, that horse ain't got no head. This man was on him whipping him, whipping, whipping, and he don't have no head. And that horse was running, and he say that scared him so bad he run, he run, he run. He is so scared he can't even tell his mama about it. When he come to his senses he mama ask, "What is the matter wid you?"

And he say, "Mama, something scared me about to death, scared me to death tonight."

"What in the world wuz it?"

Then he tell what happen. From that to this you can't tell Sonny there ain't no ghoses. He say, "I saw and I heard it, scared me about to death." (B17).

—*Susie Brooks.*

THE END

Notes and Bibliography

SYMBOLS: In this Notes and Bibliography *A1, A2, A3* etc. are used to identify sources; for example, *A1* is Allen, Minnie Hollowell; *WA* signifies White American; *BA* Black American; *AI* American Indian; and *J* Juvenile or under 16 years of age.

A1—Allen, Minne Hollowell, WA, Winsteadville, Beaufort County, North Carolina.

A2—Andrews, Bruce, WA, Bladen County, N. C., Route 2, Ivanhoe, N. C., native of Cumberland County, N. C.

A3—Ansell, Henry B., *Recollections of a Knotts Island Boyhood*, "North Carolina Folklore," Vol. VII, July 1959.

A4—The Associated Press.

A5—Artis, Maggie, BA, Boykins, Southampton County, Virginia.

A6—Askew, Robert, WA, Ahoskie, Hertford County, N. C.

B1—Baccus, Emily M., *Negro Folk Stories*, "Journal of American Folk Lore," IX, p. 228.

B2—Bacon, Miss A. M., and Parsons, Mrs. E. C., *Folklore From Elizabeth City County, Virginia*, "Journal of American Folk Lore," XXXV, 1922.

B3—Bailey, Rocky, BA-J, Como, Hertford County, N. C.

B4—Baker, Memry, after Jacob Crouse, North Carolina WPA Writers Project, 1938, N. C. Archives, Box 19.

B5—Banks, E. P., WA, Murfreesboro, Hertford County, N. C.

B6—Barber, W. P., BA, Free Union, Jamesville, Martin County, North Carolina.

B7—Barnes, Spencer, WA, Jackson, Northampton County, N. C.

B8—Barton, Lew, AI, *Me-Told Tales Among the Lumbee*, "North Carolina Folklore," XIX, September 1971.

B9—Berry, Joseph, Manteo, Dare County, North Carolina.

D10—Beverly, Edward, BA, Murfreesboro, N. C., native of Winton, Hertford County, N. C.

B11—Beverly, Robert, *The History and Present State of Virginia*, 1705, Charlottesville reprint, 1968.

B12—Black, V. L., WA, Route 5, Franklin, Macon County, N. C., native of Florida, several years in West Indies.

B13—Blanchard, Ruth (Mrs. Lucius), Ahoskie, Hertford County, N. C., native of Perquimans County, N. C.

B13a—Boggs, Ralph Steele, *North Carolina Folk Tales Current in 1820s,* "Journal of American Folk Lore, XLVII, p. 86.

B14—Boone, Sam, WA, Chapel Hill, Orange County, N. C., native of Gates County, N. C.

B15—Boyd, William K. ed., *William Byrd's Histories of the Dividing Line Betwixt Virginia and North Carolina,* N. C. Historical Commission, Raleigh, 1929.

B16—Brickell, John, *Natural History of North Carolina,* Dublin, 1737, N. C. Public Libraries reprint, 1911, Johnson, Murfreesboro, N. C., reprint, 1968.

B17—Brooks, Susie Mae, BA, Newsons, Southampton County, Va., native of Murfreesboro, N. C.

B18—Brown, Carol Smith (Mrs. Howard), WA, Murfreesboro, Hertford County, N. C., native of Scotland County, N. C.

B19—The Frank C. Brown Collection of *North Carolina Folklore,* 5 vols., Duke University, Durham.

B20—Bruce, P. A., *Institutional History of Virginia in the Seventeenth Century,* New York and London, I, 1919.

B21—Burgess, Herbert, WA, Murfreesboro, Hertford County, N.C.

B22—Byrne, Patrick, *Irish Ghost Stories,* Cork, 1965.

C1—Cahoon, David, WA, Bath, Beaufort County, N. C.

C2—Chambers, R., *Popular Rhymes of Scotland,* p. 184.

C3—Choppin, Roy, Wake County, N. C., 1928 informant for N. C. WPA Writers Project, 1938, N. C. Archives, Box 19.

C4—Clark, Joseph D., *North Carolina Superstitions,* "North Carolina Folklore," XIV, July 1966.

C5—Colvin, Margaret (Mrs. Albert H.), St. Mary's County, Maryland, native of Washington, D. C.

C6—Cooper, Horton, *North Carolina Mountain Folklore and Miscellany.,* 1972, Johnson Publishing Co., Murfreesboro, N. C.

C7—Corbitt, David L., ed., *Explorations, Description and Attempted Settlements of Carolina, 1584-1590,* N. C. Archives, Raleigh, 1953.

C8—Corbett, Evelyn Johnson (Mrs. Hill), WA, Jacksonville, Onslow County, N. C., native of Bladen County, N. C.

C9—Cowan, Dot Ainsley (Mrs. Jack), WA, Murfreesboro, Hertford County, N. C., native of Tyrrell County, N. C.

C10—Cross, Tom Peete, *Witchcraft in North Carolina,* "Studies in Philology," XVI, July, 1919, no. 3, pp. 217-287.

C11—Crouse, Herbert, WA, Elizabeth City, Pasquotank County, N. C., native of Whitesburg, Letcher County, Kentucky.

D1—Davis, H. C., *Negro Folklore in South Carolina*, "Journal of American Folk Lore, XXVIII, p. 248.
D2—Davis, Hubert J., *The Great Dismal Swamp, Its History, Folklore and Science*, Johnson Publ., Murfreesboro, 1971.
D3—Davis, Ralph, Murfreesboro, Hertford County, N. C., native of Northampton County, N. C.
D4—Dillard, Richard, *Legends of Eastern North Carolina*, Edenton, N. C., printed for the author, 1926.
D5—Dorson, Richard M., *America Begins*, Pantheon Books, 1950.
D6—Dromgoole, Littleton, BA, Murfreesboro, Hertford County, N. C., native of Brunswick County, Virginia.

E1—Eby, Cecil D., Jr., ed., *The Old South Illustrated*, by Porte Crayon (David Hunter Strother), Chapel Hill, 1959.
E2—Eliot, John, *New England Historical and Genealogical Register*, XXXV, 1881.
E3—Everett, Elvis, BA-J, Murfreesboro, Hertford County, N. C.
E4—Everett, Queenie, BA, Murfreesboro, Hertford County, N. C.

F1—Felton, Billy, WA, Eure, Gates County, N. C.
F2—Ferguson, Doris (Mrs. Fenton), Murfreesboro, N. C., native of Snow Hill, Greene County, N. C.
F3—Foster, Ann, *The Examination and Confession of Ann Foster*, "Salem Witchcrafts."
F4—Foutz, C. B., WA, Newsoms, Virginia, native of Bonsak, Roanoke County, Virginia.
F5—Fulford, A. Dean, Pamlico Beach, Beaufort County, N. C.
F6—Fulford, Mrs. Junius C., WA, Pamlico Beach, Beaufort County, N. C.
F7—Futrell, Horace, BA, Murfreesboro, Hertford County, N. C.

G1—Gates, Theophilus, *The Travels, Experience, Exercises of the Mind and First Travels of Theophilus R. Gates*, Philadelphia, 1818, Washburn reprint, Charlotte, 1949.
G2—Glendenning, William, *Life*, for the author, Philadelphia, Pa. 1795.
G3—Goodrich, Addie, WA, Surry County, Va., R 1, Wakefield.
G4—Grant, W. Stewart, *Popular Superstitions of the Highlanders of Scotland*, Edinburgh, 1823, Ward Lock reprint, 1970.

G5—Gray, Thomas R., *The Confession of Nat Turner*, Baltimore 1831; Johnson, F. Roy, *The Nat Turner Slave Insurrection with Gray's Confessions*, pp. 225-248.

G6—Green, June, BA, Occoneechee Neck, Northampton County, North Carolina.

G7—Green, Paul, *Words and Ways, stories and incidents from my Cape Fear Valley Folklore Collection*, N. C. Folklore Society, 1968.

G8—Griffith, S. Louis, WA, Murfreesboro, Hertford County, N. C.

G9—Gunmore, A. M., *Witchcraft and Quakerism*, Philadelphia and London, 1908.

10—Gyles, John, *Memoirs of Old Adventures, Strange Deliverances &c.* in the "Captivity of John Gyles esq., Commander of the Garrison on St. George's River," photostat Americana, 2d series, Boston, 1936.

H1—Hall, A. C., Jr., WA, Wake Forest, Wake County, N. C.

H2—Hall, Clement, *A Collection of Many Christian Experiences, Sentences, and Several Places of Scripture Improved*, New Bern, 1753; N. C. Archives reprint, 1961, with introduction by William S. Powell.

H3—Hawks, Francis L., *History of North Carolina, 1663-1728*, Fayetteville, N. C., 1858.

H4—Hatcher, William E., *Life of J. B. Jester, D. D.*, Baltimore, 1887.

H5—Henderson, William, *Folk Lore of the Northern Counties of England and the Borders*, London, 1866, reprint Rowman and Littlefield, Totowa, N. J., 1973.

I1—Ireland, John, WA, Hobucken, Pamlico County, N. C.

J1—Johnson, Alex, BA, Route 3, Ahoskie, Hertford County, N. C., native of Halifax County, N. C., several years a resident of Marianna, Florida.

J2—Johnson, Dean, WA, Lake Creek Township, Bladen County, N. C., Route 2, Ivanhoe, N. C.

J3—Johnson, F. Roy, *The Algonquians*, 2 vols., Murfreesboro, N. C., 1972.

J4—Johnson, F. Roy, *The Fabled Doctor Jim Jordan*, Murfreesboro, 1963.

J5—Johnson, F. Roy, *The Nat Turner Story*, Murfreesboro, 1971.

J6—Johnson, F. Roy, *The Tuscaroras*, 2 vols., Murfreesboro, 1967.

J7—Johnson, F. Roy, *Witches and Demons in History and Folklore*, Murfreesboro, 1968.

J8—Johnson, Guions Griffis, *Ante-Bellum North Carolina*, Chapel Hill, 1937.

J9—Johnson, Guion Griffis, *Revival Movement in Ante-bellum North Carolina*, "North Carolina Historical Review," vol. X, 1933.

J10—Johnson, John F., Lake Creek Township, Bladen County, North Carolina.

J11—Johnson, Mary (Mrs. Alex), BA, Route 3, Ahoskie, Hertford County, N. C., native of Gates County, N. C.

J12—Johnson, Nolon K., WA, Lake Creek Township, Bladen County, N. C., Route 2, Ivanhoe, N. C.

J13—Jordan, McCoy, BA-J, Como, Hertford County, N. C.

J14—Jordan, Tom, BA, Murfreesboro, Hertford County, native of Plantersville, S. C., raised in Isle of Wight County, Va.

J15—Josselyn, John, *New England's Rareties Discovered*, 1672, Edward Tuckerman, "Transactions and Collections of the American Antiquarian Society: Archaelogia Americana," IV, 1860.

K1—Kennedy, Mrs. W. E., WA, Norfolk, Va., native of Nansemond County, Va.

K2—Knott, Father Edward, *Escape from the Deep*, in "Narratives of Early Maryland," Letter of 1638, 122.

L1—Lane, Oscar, WA, Whaleyville, Va., native of Gates County, North Carolina.

L2—Lawson, John, *Lawson's History of North Carolina*, Garrett and Massie, Richmond, 1951.

L3—Lassiter, Mrs. Harvey, BA, Route 1, Woodland, Hertford County, N. C.

L4—Leather, E. M., *Folklore of Hertfordshire*.

L5—Lee, Joyce, WA, Murfreesboro, Hertford County, N. C., native of Southampton County, Va.

L6—Lemmon, Sarah McCulloh, ed., *The Pettigrew Papers*, I, 1685-1818, N. C. Archives, 1971.

L7—Lewis, Rev. R. R., BA, Winton, Hertford County, N. C.

L8—Liverman, Irma, WA, Route 2, Ahoskie, Hertford County, North Carolina.

M1—Marable, William I, WA, Chowan College, Hertford County, N. C., native of Lunenburg County, Va.

M2—Mather, Cotton, *Magnalia Christi Americana;* or *The Ecclesiastical History of New-England from its first planting in the year 1620, unto the year of our Lord 1698,* 2 vols., Hartford, 1853-1855.

M3—Mather, Cotton, *The Wonders of the Invisible World,* Library of Old Authors, London, 1862.

M4—Mayo, J. A., WA, Alliance, Pamlico County, N. C., native of Hobuken, N. C.

M5—McCullen, J. T., Jr., and Jeri Tanner, *The Devil Outwitted in Folklore and Literature,* "North Carolina Folklore," XVII, May 1969, p. 18.

M6—McMillan, Douglas J., *The Vanishing Hitchhiker in Eastern North Carolina,* "North Carolina Folklore, XX, Aug. 1873.

M7—Mizelle, Judy (Mrs. Ernest), WA, Rich Square, Northampton County, N. C., native of Ahoskie, Hertford County, N. C.

M8—Mooney, James, *Myths of the Cherokee and Sacred Formulas of the Cherokees,* 19th Annual Report, B.A.E., Washington, D. C.

M9—Moore, Claude H., *The Ghosts of Fryar's Bridge,* ."The State," XXXXI, March 1974.

M10—Moore, Dallas, BA, Murfreesboro, Hertford County, N. C., native of Northampton County, N. C.

M11—Moore, Ivan, WA, Murfreesboro, Hertford County, N. C., native of Sayres Neck, Cumberland County, New Jersey.

M12—Moore, Jimmy, WA, Route 4, Ahoskie, Hertford County, North Carolina.

M13—Morgan, Mrs. Nora, WA, Eure, Gates County, N. C.

M14—Murphy, Henry C., ed., *Memoirs of the Long Island Historical Society,* I, Brooklyn, 1867, translated from Danckaerts' and Sluyeter, *Journal of a Voyage to New York and a Tour of Several of the American Colonies in 1679-1680.*

NCCR—Saunders, William E., ed., *Colonial Records of North Carolina,* Trustees of Public Libraries, 10 vols.

NCSR—Clark, Walter, ed., *State Records of North Carolina,* Trustees of Public Libraries, 16 vols.

NCHCR—Parker, Mattie Erma Edwards, ed., *North Carolina Higher Court Records,* vols. I and II.

N1—*Narratives of Early Maryand,* Letter of 1642, pp. 137-139.

O1—Owen, Guy, WA, N. C. State U. at Raleigh, native of Bladen County, N. C.

P1—Parsons, Elsie Clew, and A. M. Bacon, *Folk-Lore from Elizabeth City County, Virginia*, "Journal of American Folk-Lore," XXX, 1917.

P2—Parsons, Elsie Clew, *Tales from Guilford County, N. C.*, "Journal of American Folk-Lore," XXX, 1917.

P3—Parsons, Elsie Clew, *The Cherokee of Robeson County*, "Journal of American Folk-Lore," XXXII.

P4—Paschal, G. W., *Morgan Edwards' Material Toward a History of the Baptists in the Province of North Carolina*, "North Carolina Historical Review," VII, July 1930.

P5—Pendleton, Louis, Negro Folk-Lore and Witchcraft in the *South*, "Journal of American Folk-Lore," II.

P6—Pendleton, Louis, *Negro Folk-Lore and Witchcraft in South Carolina*, "Journal of American Folk Lore," III, 206.

P7—Perry, Mrs. Tray Jenette, WA, Colerain, Bertie County, N. C.

P8—Peterson, Gertrude Johnson (Mrs. Fennel), WA, Kelly, Bladen County, N. C.

P9—Pierce, Andrew, BA, Free Union, Jamesville, Martin County, North Carolina.

P10—Pipkin, Lollie Ruth Sewell (Mrs. G. H.), WA, Murfreesboro, Hertford County, N. C.

P11—*The Pirates and the Palatines*, "North Carolina Folklore," VI, pp. 23-26.

P12—Porter, Doc, BA, Murfreesboro, Hertford County, N. C.

P13—Porter, Jasper, BA-J, Como, Hertford County, N. C.

P14—Powell, William S., *The Devil in North Carolina*, "The State," April 10, 1954.

P15—Powell, William S., *The N.C. Gazeteer*, Chapel Hill, 1968.

P16—Pridgen, Carey, BA, Lake Creek Township, Bladen County, N. C., Route 2, Ivanhoe, N. C.

P17—Puckett, N. N., *Folk Beliefs of the Southern Negro*, Chapel Hill, 1926.

P18—Pugh, Jessie F., WA, Elizabeth City, Pasquotank County, N. C., native of Camden County, N. C.

R1—Rivers, Charles Leonard, BA-J, Como, Hertford County, N.C.

R2—Roberts, Nathan, Currituck County, N. C.

R3—Ross, James, *Life and Times of Elder Reuben Ross*.

R4—Rudwin, Maximilian, *The Devil in Legend and Literature*, Open Court, La Salle, Ill., 1931.

R5—Russell, Noadiah, *Diary of, 1682-1684*, "New England Genealogical Register," VII, 1853.

S1—Sawyer, Lem, *Blackbeard, a Comedy in Four Parts, Founded on Fact,* Washington, 1824, reprint with introduction by Richard Walser, N. C. Archives, 1952.
S2—Sexton, J. W., Winton, Hertford County, N. C., native of Lake Phelps, Washington County, N. C.
S3—Sharpe, Bill, *A New Geography of North Carolina,* Raleigh, 4 vols, 1954-1965.
S4—Shaw, Jim, BA, Route 1, Boykins, Southampton County, Va., native of Hoke County, N. C.
S5—Sikes, W. Wirt, *British Goblins,* London, 1880
S6—Smallwood, Noah, BA, Route 2, Ahoskie, Hertford County, N. C., native of Indian Woods, Bertie County, N. C.
S7—Smith, Claude, WA, Murfreesboro, Hertford County, N. C., native of Rich Square, Northampton County, N. C.
S8—Snead, Wesley, BA-J, Murfreesboro, Hertford County, N. C.
S9—Spence E. B., WA, Pendleton, Northampton County, N. C.
S11—*Sprunt, James, Historical Monographs,* University of North Carolina, 1904, IV, 130.
S12—St. Clair, Shelia, *Folklore of the Ulster People,* Cork, 1971.
S13—Sturgill, Virgil, Asheville, N. C.
S14—Stewart, W. Grant, *Popular Superstitions of the Highlands of Scotland,* Edinburgh, 1823.
S15—Stutts, J. C., N. C. WPA Writers Project, 1938, N. C. Archives, Box 19; "North Carolina Folklore," XIX, Jan. 1971.

T1—Turner, Mrs. O. C., WA, Gatesville, Gates County, N. C.
T3—Tyner, Andrew J., BA, Murfreesboro, Hertford County, N. C., native of Northampton County, N. C.
T3—Taylor, R. S., WA, Eure, Gates County, N. C.

V1—Vann, Linwood Earl, WA, Murfreesboro, Hertford County, North Carolina.
V2—Vann, Richard T., WA, Murfreesboro, Hertford County, N.C.
V3—Vaughan, Jack, WA, Northampton County, N. C., native of Halifax County, N. C.
V4—Vaughan, Mrs. Jack, WA, Northampton County, N. C., native of Lexington, S. C.
V5—Vaughan, Jim Allen, BA, Menola, Hertford County, N. C.
V6—Vaughan, John, BA-J, Murfreesboro, Hertford County, N. C.
V7—Vaughan, Wash, BA, Northampton County, N. C.

V8—Vaughan, W. L., after S. F. Freeman, who as a boy worked at Diamond City sawmill, Martin County. N. C. WPA Writers Project, 1938, N. C. Archives, Box 19.

W1—Wagoner, Dorothy Hand (Mrs. Jim), Murfreesboro, Hertford County, N. C., native of Gates County, N. C.
W2—Walser, Richard, *Old Christmas at Rodanthe*, "North Caroline Folklore," X, 1.
W3—Warren, Mary Dyson (Mrs. J. Dusty), Murfreesboro, Hertford County, N. C., native of New Jersey.
W4—Watson, Charlie, Murfreesboro, Hertford County, N. C.
W5—Weathersbee, *The Devil's Rock*, "North Carolina Folklore, XVI, 1.
W6-Webster, Ronald, WA, Bath, Beaufort County, N. C.
W7—Whedbee, Charles H., *Legends of the Outer Banks*, Blair, Winston-Salem, 1966.
W8—Whitley, Randolph, WA, Murfreesboro, Hertford County, North Carolina.
W9—White, Mrs. R. Kelly, WA, Conway, Northampton County, N. C., native of Hertford County, N. C.
W10—Wiggins, Clayton, WA, Murfreesboro, N. C., native of Edgecombe County, N. C.
W11—Wiggins, R. S., Murfreesboro, N. C., LeGrange, Lenoir County, N. C.
W12—Wiggins, Tony, BA-J, Como, Hertford County, N. C.
W13—Williams, Shelton, BA-J, Murfreesboro, Hertford County, North Carolina.
W14—Winthrop, John, *Journal*, "History of New England, 1630-1648," James Kendall Hosmer, ed., 2 vols, Scribners, 1908.
W15—Woodley, James Kelly, BA, Boykins, Southampton County, Virginia, native of Sussex County, Va.

Y1—Yeates Tom, BA, Acorn Hill, Gates County, N. C.
Y2—York, Brantley, *Autobiography*, "John Lawson Monographs of the Trinity College Historical Society," Durham, 1910, I.

Index

A
Apparitions, 139-148, 169-186.

B
Banshee, The, 139, 143-152.
Barguest, The, 139.
Bear, The, 58.
*Blackbeard, 45, 46, 48, 62, 68.
*Blackbeard's ship, 45-48.
Black Snake, The, 59.
Black arts, 129, 130.
Blasphemy, 34-39.
Bloody Bones, The, 57.
Bluebeard, 62.
Bogies, The, 9, 57, 68.
Brimstone, 36, 75, 94.
Brownies, The, 68, 113.
Buried alive, 171.

C
Children in folklore, 53-68.
Children's frights, 53-68.
Churches, 11-12.
Clergymen; see Preachers.
Coach Whip, The, 58, 78.

D
Davis, James, 12.
Dead Bells, 148-149.
Defiling Sabbath, 75-78, 110-112.
Demons, 46-48, 54, 57-61, 66, 109, 110, 113-115, 116-118, 121-130.
Death described, 155-165.
Dead, messages from, 166-170.
Devil children, 20, 21, 23-24.
Devil's Horse, The., 59.

DEVIL, The:

accosts Christian, 108.
aid sought by parents, 68.
aliases of, 53-56, 66, 69, 100, 133.
as a trickster, 83, 87.
as Bad Man, 56.
as Old Bad Boy, 56.
as Old Black Boy, 55.
as Old Black Sambo, 55.
as Old Hob, 56.
as Old Red Eyes, 55.
as Old Scratch, 53-54.
as Prince of Darkness, 55.
as Prince of Fright, 55.
attends church, 87-88.
challenges preachers, 87-89.
claims his own, 34-35, 65-85.
controls of, 72, 108, 109, 110, 191.
described, 14, 21, 23, 53-56, 59, 65-68, 77, 78, 81, 84, 86, 91, 95, 112.
fear of, 13, 155.
fisherman catches, 110-112.
funned, 91-98.
imps of, 57, 155.
importance of, 65-68.
Indian, 67.
in England, 66.
in North Carolina, 10.
in proverbs, 65.
lumbering of, 86, 160.
music box of, 106-107.
outwitted, 99-108.
pitch fork of, 81.
popularity of, 65, 68.
sting of, 85-86.
voice of, 86.

Dogs as death portent, 149-50, 151, 165.
Doughface, The, 61.

E

Eagle, The, 59.
Easter, Rev. John, 13, 133.
Eliot, Rev. John, 13, 133.
Evil spirits; see Demons.

F

Fairies, The, 9, 68, 113-115.
Fairy musicians, 113 115.
Falling picture, 152-153.
Fiddlers' Green, 103.
Flying Head, The, 61.
Folk culture, 9-10, 12.
FOLKLORE:
    development of, 12.
    influence of travelers and preachers on, 12.
    in North Carolina, 9-10, 65.
    religious, 13.
Folk tale, popularity of, 12, 14.
Fortune telling, 14.
Frog, The, 127.

G

Gabriel Hounds, The, 144, 151.
Garcia, Rev. John, 11.
Gates, Theophilus, 67.
Ghost laying, 46, 136, 196, 201, 202, 222, 224, 231.
Ghost-seeing, 14, 195.
Ghostly humor, 234-241.
Ghost tale popularity, 14, 68.

GHOSTS:
    as animals, 183, 186.
    as guardians of living, 172-186.
    as craving spriits, 203-213
    as lights, 167, 169, 194, 212, 216, 228, 229-230.
    as scary spirits, 214-221.
    as treasure guardians, 223-233.
    behavior of, 162-163, 177, 180, 183, 184-186, 189-195, 205-208, 209-210, 212, 223-230, 231, 235, 240.
    cause insanity, 182.
    converse with living, 171.
    forms of, 125, 128, 167, 169, 194, 199, 201, 204, 205-208, 216, 217.
    magic of, 196-201, 223-227.
    punish living, 184, 195.
    power over living, 187-195.
Glendenning, Rev. Wm., 67-68.
Goblins; see Hobgoblins.
God, wrath of, 14, 17.
Great Awakening, 13, 17.
Great Revival, The, 17.

H

Haunted houses, 14, 202, 207-208, 212, 213, 217, 230, 233, 236.
Ha'nts; see Ghosts.
Hell, described, 91-92.
    carried to, 21, 24.
Hell fire, 133-136.
Hell Hounds, The, 57, 69.
Hobgoblins, 9, 57.
Hoop Snake, The, 58, 78.
Human monsters, 59, 61.

I

Imps of the Devil, 57, 155.
Indian tales, 132-133.
Irving, Washington, 68.

J

Jack-o'-lantern, 14, 116, 121.
James, Jesse, 62.
Jeter, Dr. J. B., 14.
Judgment, day of, 69.

K

Kill Devil Hill, 100.
Knott, Father Edward, 156.

L
Lawson, John, 9, 53, 67, 133.
Lowry outlaws, 121.
Luther, Martin, 66.

M
Mather, Cotton, 43, 66, 166.
Money rod, 225, 227.
Monster children, 18-24,
Monsters, Indian, 58.

O
Old Buck, 57.
Old Hairy Man, The, 61.
Old saints, 156.
Owl, The, 150, 160.

P
Palatines, ship of, 49-51.
Panther, The, 58.
Pierpont, Rev. James, 43.
Pigseys, The, 122.
Plat-Eye, The, 116, 124, 126.
Portents of death, 139-152.
Preachers, itinerant, 10, 11, 12, 155.
  Anglican, 10, 11.

PROVIDENCE.
  acts of nature, 40-42.
  discloses mysteries, 43-51.
  God acts through, 13, 20, 155
  Judgments of, 29-41.
  messages of, 25-33.
  threat of, 12, 20, 155.
  workings of, 17-18.

Q
Quincy, Josiah, 12.
Queen Anne's Revenge, 46.

R
Raleigh's Spectre Ship, 43, 45.
Rattan vine, 136.
Rattle Snake, The, 133.
Raw Head, The, 57.
Rooster, The, 152.
Russell, Noahdiah, 44.

S
Sawyer, Lem, 68.
Scarecrow, The, 55.
Second-sight, 129, 221.
Shike Poke, The, 59.
Silkie, 116.
Spectre at Lynn, 44-45.
Spirit magic, 46-48, 72, 81, 83, 100-101, 104, 112, 123, 127-128, 129-131, 133-136, 167, 169, 189-191, 192-193, 204.

T
Talking in tongues, 13.
Teach, Edward; see Blackbeard.
Thunderbolt, The, 35-36.
Trances, 13.
Turkey Buzzard, The, 59.
Turner, Nat, 62.

W
Water Monster, The, 58.
Weather signs, 94.
Werewolf, 221-222.
Whistling Snake, The, 131-132.
Wild Man, The, 61.
Will-o'-wisp, 122.
Winthrop, John, 18, 31.
Witches, 9, 61, 66, 115.
Witchcraft, 14, 155.
Witch trials, 60.
Wizardry, 129, 136, 202, 225.
Wolf, The, 58.
Woodman, Mr., 13.
Wraith, The, 139-143.